## 'You're asking me to come as your date?'

'That's right.'

A date. A party. With this man. Selene had never done anything like that in her life.

She couldn't possibly say yes, even though she wanted to more than she'd ever wanted anything in her life.

On the other hand, why not?

For virtually the first time in her life she was free to make her own decision about something. Feeling liberated, she opened her mouth. 'I don't have anything to wear.'

'That's easily solved.'

'Would we drink champagne?'

Stefan's mouth curved into a smile so sexy it should have been illegal. 'All night.'

'And would we—?'

The devil danced in his eyes and his mouth moved fractionally closer to hers. 'Yes, we definitely would.'

*USA TODAY* bestselling author **Sarah Morgan** writes lively, sexy stories for both Mills & Boon® Modern™ Romance and Medical Romance™.

As a child Sarah dreamed of being a writer, and although she took a few interesting detours on the way she is now living that dream. With her writing career she has successfully combined business with pleasure, and she firmly believes that reading romance is one of the most satisfying and fat-free escapist pleasures available. Her stories are unashamedly optimistic, and she is always pleased when she receives letters from readers saying that her books have helped them through hard times.

*RT Book Reviews* has described her writing as 'action-packed and sexy', and nominated her books for their Reviewer's Choice Awards and their 'Top Pick' slot. In 2012 Sarah received the prestigious RITA® Award from the Romance Writers of America for her book *Doukakis's Apprentice*.

Sarah lives near London with her husband and two children, who innocently provide an endless supply of authentic dialogue. When she isn't writing or reading Sarah enjoys music, movies, and any activity that takes her outdoors.

Readers can find out more about Sarah and her books from her website: www.sarahmorgan.com. She can also be found on Facebook and Twitter.

**Recent titles by the same author:**

WOMAN IN A SHEIKH'S WORLD
 *(The Private Lives of Public Playboys)*
A NIGHT OF NO RETURN
 *(The Private Lives of Public Playboys)*
THE FORBIDDEN FERRARA
ONCE A FERRARA WIFE…

**Did you know these are also available as eBooks?**
**Visit www.millsandboon.co.uk**

# SOLD TO THE ENEMY

BY
SARAH MORGAN

First published in Great Britain 2013
by Mills & Boon, an imprint of Harlequin (UK) Limited.
Harlequin (UK) Limited, Eton House, 18-24 Paradise Road,
Richmond, Surrey TW9 1SR

© Sarah Morgan 2013

ISBN: 978 0 263 23409 1

Harlequin (UK) policy is to use papers that are natural, renewable and recyclable products and made from wood grown in sustainable forests. The logging and manufacturing process conform to the legal environmental regulations of the country of origin.

Printed and bound in Great Britain
by CPI Antony Rowe, Chippenham, Wiltshire

# SOLD TO THE ENEMY

# CHAPTER ONE

'No ONE will lend you money, Selene. They are all too afraid of your father.'

'Not all.' Selene sat down on the bed and stroked her mother's hair—hair tended regularly by hairdressers in order to keep up the appearance of a perfect life. 'Stop worrying. I'm going to get you away from here.'

Her mother lay still. She said 'from here' but they both knew that what she really meant was 'from him'.

'I should be the one saying that to you. I should have left years ago. When I first met your father he was so charming. Every woman in the room wanted him and he only had eyes for me. Have you any idea how that feels?'

Selene opened her mouth to say *How could I, when I've been trapped on this island for most of my life?* but realised that would only hurt her mother more. 'I can imagine it must have been very exciting. He was rich and powerful.' She wouldn't make that mistake. She would never let love blind her to the true nature of the man underneath.

'It's stupid to talk of leaving when we both know he'll never let us go. As far as the world is concerned we're the perfect family. He isn't going to let anything ruin that image.' Her mother rolled away, turning her face to the wall.

Selene felt a rush of frustration. It was like watching

someone adrift on a raft, making no effort to save themselves. 'We're not going to ask him. It's our decision. *Ours.* Maybe it's time we told the world this "family" is a lie.'

Her mother's lack of response didn't surprise her. Her father had dictated to them and controlled them for so long she'd forgotten she even had a choice.

Despite the oppressive summer heat and the fact that their fortress home had no air-conditioning, a chill spread across her skin and ran deep into her bones.

How many years did it take, she wondered, before you no longer believed your life was worth fighting for? How many years before hope turned to helplessness, before anger became acceptance and spirit was beaten to a stupor? How many years until she, too, chose to lie on her side facing the wall rather than stand up and face the day?

Beyond the closed shutters that blotted out the only window in the tiny bedroom the sun beamed its approval from a perfect blue sky onto the sparkling Mediterranean, its brightness a cruel contrast to the darkness inside the room.

To many, the Greek Islands were paradise. Perhaps some of them were. Selene didn't know. She only knew this one, and Antaxos was no paradise. Cut off from its neighbours by a stretch of dangerous sea, rocks that threatened ships like the jaws of a monster and by the fearsome reputation of the man who owned it, this island was closer to hell than heaven.

Selene tucked the covers around her mother's thin shoulders. 'Leave everything to me.'

That statement injected her mother with an energy that nothing else could. 'Don't make him angry.'

She'd heard those words more often than she could count.

She'd spent her life tiptoeing around 'angry'.

'You don't have to live like this, watching everything

you say and everything you do because of him.' Looking at her mother, Selene felt sad. Once, she'd been a beauty and it had been that blonde, Nordic beauty that had attracted the attention of the rich playboy Stavros Antaxos. Her mother had been dazzled by wealth and power and she'd melted under his charm like candle wax under a hot flame, never seeing the person beneath the smooth sophistication.

One bad choice, Selene thought. Her mother had made one bad choice and then spent years living with it, her heart and spirit crushed by a life spent with a ruthless man.

'Let's not talk about him. I had an e-mail this week from Hot Spa in Athens.' She'd been nursing the news for days, not daring to share it before now. 'Remember I told you about them? It's a really upmarket chain. And they have spa hotels on Crete, Corfu and Santorini. I sent them samples of my candles and my soap and they *love* them. They used them in their treatment rooms and three of their top clients insisted on taking them home and paid a fortune for the privilege. Now they want to talk to me and put in a large order. It's the break I've been hoping for.' She was buzzing inside and longing to share the excitement so it came as a blow when her mother's only response was to shake her head.

'He'll never let you do it.'

'I don't need his permission to live my life the way I want to live it.'

'And how are you going to live it? You need money to set up your business and he won't give you money that enables us to leave him.'

'I know. Which is why I don't intend to ask him. I have another plan.' She'd learned not to speak without first checking to see who might be listening and instinctively she turned her head to see that the door was closed, even though this was her mother's bedroom and she'd se-

cured the door herself. Even though *he* wasn't even on
the island. 'I'm leaving tonight and I'm telling you this
because I won't be able to contact you for a few days and
I don't want you to worry about me. As far as everyone
is concerned I am at the convent for my usual week of re-
treat and meditation.'

'How can you leave? Even if you could slip past his security and make it off the island you will be recognised.
Someone will call him and he will be furious. You know
how obsessed he is about maintaining the image of the
perfect family.'

'One of the advantages of being the shy, reclusive
daughter of a man feared by everyone is that no one is
expecting to see me. But just to cover all eventualities I
have a disguise.' And she didn't intend to share the details
with anyone. Not even her mother, who was now looking
at her with panic in her eyes.

'And if you do manage to make it as far as the main-
land, what then? Have you thought that far?'

'Yes, I've thought that far.' And further, much further,
to a future that was nothing like the past. 'You don't need
to know any of this. All you need to do is trust me and wait
for me to return and fetch you. I'd take you now only two
of us travelling together are more likely to attract attention. You have to stay here and keep up the perfect family
pretence for just a little longer. Once I have the money and
somewhere to stay I'm coming back for you.'

Her mother gripped her arm tightly. 'If by any chance
you manage to do this, you should not come back. It's too
late for me.'

'It drives me mad when you say things like that.' Selene
hugged her mother. 'I will come back. And then we're
leaving together and he can find someone else to control.'

'I wish I had money to give you.'

*So did she.* If her mother had maintained her independence then perhaps they wouldn't be in this mess now, but her father's first and cleverest move following his marriage had been to ensure his wife had no income of her own, thus making her dependent on him in every way. Her mother had confessed that at first she'd found it romantic to have a man who wanted to care for her. It had been later, much later, that she'd realised that he hadn't wanted to care for her. He'd wanted to control her. And so her mother's independence had slowly leeched away, stolen not by a swift kill but by a slow, cruel erosion of her confidence.

'I have enough to get me to Athens. Then I'm going to get a loan to start my business.' It was the only option open to her and she knew other people did it all the time. They borrowed money and they paid it back and she would pay it back, too. All of it.

'He has contacts at all the banks. None of them will loan you money, Selene.'

'I know. Which is why I'm not going to a bank.'

Her mother shook her head. 'Name one person who would be prepared to do business with you. Show me a man with the guts to stand up to your father and I'll show you a man who doesn't exist.'

'He exists.' Her heart pumped hard against her chest and she forced herself to breathe slowly. 'There is one man who isn't afraid of anyone or anything. A strong man.'

'Who?'

Selene kept her voice casual. 'I'm going to see Stefanos Ziakas.'

The name alone drained the colour from her mother's face. 'Ziakas is another version of your father. He's a ruthless, self-seeking playboy with no conscience and not one shred of gentleness in him. Don't be fooled by that handsome face and that charismatic smile. He's deadly.'

'No, he isn't. I met him once, years ago, on the yacht on one of the occasions we were forced to play "happy families" in public. He was kind to me.' Selene was annoyed to feel herself blushing.

'If he was kind, it was because he knew it would annoy your father. They hate each other.'

'He didn't know who I was when we started talking.'

'You were the only seventeen-year-old there. It was obvious who you were.' Her mother sounded weary. 'Ask yourself why a sophisticated man like him would spend his time talking to you when he came with the actress Anouk Blaire.'

'He told me she was boring. He said she only cared about how she looked and who wrote about her and that being with him enhanced her career. He said I was much more interesting. We talked all night.' About everything. She'd told him things she'd never told anyone before. Not about her family, of course—she was too well trained to let that particular truth slip—but she'd talked about her dreams and her hopes for the future and been grateful when he hadn't laughed. He'd listened with those sexy eyes fixed on her and when she'd asked him if he thought she might be able to run a business one day he'd spoken words she'd never forgotten.

*You can do anything if you want it enough.*

Well, she wanted it.

Her mother sighed. 'The schoolgirl and the billionaire. And because of this one conversation you think he'll help you?'

*Come back in five years, Selene Antaxos, then maybe we'll talk.*

She'd wanted to do a whole lot more than talk and she suspected he'd known that, just as she suspected he'd guessed the truth about the fabricated life she led. She'd felt more of a connection with him than she had with any other human being. For the first time in her life someone had listened to her and his words had stayed with her, day and night. When life had grown hard it had been a comfort to remember that she had someone to go to if things were desperate.

And things *were* desperate.

'He'll help me.'

'That man is more likely to hurt you than help you. You have no experience of men like him. I would not put you with a man like Ziakas. I would find you someone kind and gentle who deserves you.'

'I don't want him to be kind or gentle. I need him to be ruthless or this isn't going to work. If he doesn't have the guts to stand up to my father then there is no hope for my plan. I want to run my own business and Ziakas knows more about how to do that than anyone. He did it all himself. He lost his parents when he was young. No one helped him. No one gave him a helping hand. And look at him now. He was a billionaire by the time he was thirty and he did that by himself.'

She found his story inspirational. If he could do it, why couldn't she?

Her mother struggled upright, finding energy from anxiety. 'Do you honestly think you'll just be able to walk up to a man like Stefan Ziakas and ask him for money? He is protected from the outside world by layers of security, just like your father. Getting an appointment with someone like him would be almost impossible, especially at short notice. Even if you could somehow find a way to leave the island undetected while your father is away, Ziakas won't see you.'

'He'll see me. And I have found a way to leave the island.' Determined not to reveal too much, and even more determined not to let her mother batter her confidence, Selene stood up. 'I will be back tomorrow, which gives us plenty of time to get far away before my father returns from—from his trip.' 'Trip' was the word they both used to describe her father's frequent absences from the island. It disgusted Selene that he didn't even bother to keep his infidelities a secret. Disgusted her more that her mother accepted them as part of the marriage deal.

She couldn't allow herself to think about what she'd do if her mother refused to leave, as she'd refused so many times before. All she knew was that she didn't want to spend anther day on Antaxos. She'd lived here all her life, trapped within its rocky shores, thirsty for a life other than the one she'd been given. She didn't want to spend another day in this 'family' pretending that everything was perfect.

The events of the last week had shown her that she had to do it sooner rather than later.

Bending down, she kissed her mother on the cheek. 'Dream about what you're going to do on the first day of your new life. You're going to laugh without worrying that the sound is going to draw his attention. You're going to paint again and people will buy those paintings, just as they used to.'

'I haven't painted for years. I don't feel the urge any more.'

'That's because he didn't like you doing anything that took you away from him.' The anger was like an energy source, giving her a determination that felt close to power. 'You're going to get your life back.'

'And if your father returns from Crete early and finds you gone? Have you thought of that?'

It was like stepping off a cliff or missing a step on the

stairs. Her heart bumped uncomfortably and she wanted
to clutch something for support. 'He won't return early.
Why would he?'

Bored out of his mind, Stefan lounged with his feet on
his desk.

Far beneath the glass cocoon that housed his corporate
headquarters, Athens was slowly waking up. Athens, a city
in trouble, licking its wounds as the world watched in wary
fascination. People encouraged him to move his base to a
different city. New York. London. Anywhere other than
the troubled Greek capital.

Stefan ignored them.

He had no intention of abandoning the place that had
allowed him to become who he was. He knew what it was
like to have everything and then lose it. He knew how it
felt to go from prosperity to poverty. He understood fear
and uncertainty. And he knew all about the effort required
to drag yourself back from the edge. It made winning all
the more satisfying and he'd won in a big way. He had
money and power.

People would have been surprised to learn the money
didn't interest him. But power? Power was different. He'd
learned at an early age that power was everything. Power
opened doors that were closed. Power turned no to yes and
stop to go. He'd learned that power was an aphrodisiac and,
when it needed to be, it was a weapon.

It was a weapon he wasn't afraid to use.

His phone rang for the tenth time in as many minutes
but he chose to ignore it.

A tap on the door disturbed his thoughts. Maria, his
PA, stood in the doorway.

Irritated by the interruption, Stefan lifted an eyebrow
in question and she pursed her lips.

'Don't give me that look. I know you don't want to be disturbed, but you're not answering your personal line.' When he still didn't answer, she sighed. 'Sonya's PA has been ringing and when you didn't answer Sonya herself called. She isn't in a good mood.'

'She is phoning to give me an update on her moods? I have marginally more interest in the weather forecast.'

'She wanted me to give you a message. She said to tell you she's not playing hostess at your party tonight until you make a decision about your relationship. Her exact words were...' Maria cleared her throat. '"Tell him it's either on or off."'

'It's off. I already told her that in words that even she should have been able to understand.' Exasperated, Stefan picked up his phone and deleted all his messages without listening to them. Even without looking he could feel Maria's censorship and he smiled. 'You've worked for me for twelve years. Why the long face?'

'Doesn't the end of a relationship *ever* bother you?'

'Never.'

'That says something about you, Stefan.'

'Yes. It says I'm good at handling break-ups. Go, me.'

'It says you don't care about the women you date!'

'I care as much as they do.'

With a despairing shake of her head, Maria cleared two empty coffee cups from his desk. 'You have your pick of women and you can't find *one* you want to settle down with? You are a success in every aspect of your life except one. Your personal life is a disaster.'

'I happen to consider my personal life an unqualified success.'

'You must want more than this from a relationship.'

'I want hot, frequent, uncomplicated sex.' He smiled

at her disapproving expression. 'I pick women who want the same thing.'

'Love would be the making of you.'

Love?

Stefan felt something slam shut inside him. He swung his legs off his desk. 'Did your job description change when I wasn't looking? Has there been some EU employment law that requires you to take charge of my private life?'

'Fine. I can take the hint. It's none of my business. I don't know why I even bother.' The cups rattled in her hand as she stalked through the door but she was back moments later. 'There's someone here to see you. Perhaps she'll be able to persuade you to get in touch with your human side.'

'She? I thought my first appointment wasn't until ten o'clock?'

'This person doesn't have an appointment, but I didn't feel comfortable turning her away.'

'Why not? I employ you to be the dragon at my door.'

'I can be dragon-like when I have to be but not when the person wanting to see you is a nun.'

'A *nun*? You have to be kidding me.'

'She says she has something urgent to discuss with you.'

Stefan gave a sardonic smile. 'If she's here to save my soul, tell her she's too late.'

'I will not. To be honest I have no idea what to say to her.'

'Any combination of words would have sufficed, providing "no" and "get out" were included.'

Maria squared her shoulders. 'I can't turn a nun away. I don't want that on my conscience.'

Stefan, who hadn't made the acquaintance of his conscience for several decades, was exasperated. 'I never saw you as gullible. Has it occurred to you she's probably a stripper?'

'I know a genuine nun's habit when I see one. And your cynicism does you no credit.'

'On the contrary, my cynicism has protected me nicely for years and will continue to do so—which is just as well given that you're turning into a soft touch.'

'I'm sorry, but there's no way I can tell a nun you won't see her. And she has a really sweet smile.' Maria's face softened momentarily and then she glared at him. 'If you want it done, you'll have to do it yourself.'

'Fine. Send her in. And then take a trip to the nearest fancy dress store and see for yourself how easy it is to hire a nun's costume.'

Clearly relieved to have offloaded that responsibility, Maria retreated, and Stefan felt a rush of irritation at the thought of an interruption that would bring him no benefit.

His irritation intensified at the sight of a nun in a black habit standing in the doorway to his office. Under the robes he could see that she was slightly built but she kept her head bowed, allowing him a single glimpse of a pale face under flowing black and white.

Unmoved by her pious attitude, Stefan leaned back in his chair and scrutinised his unwanted visitor. 'If you're expecting me to confess my sins then I should probably tell you that my next appointment is in an hour and that is nowhere near long enough for me to tell you all the bad things I've done in my life. On the other hand if you're about to beg for cash then you should know that all my charitable donations are handled through my lawyers, via a separate part of my company. I just make the money. I leave other people to spend it.'

The tone he used would have had most people backing towards the door but she simply closed it so that they were alone.

'There is no need to close the door,' he said coldly, 'because you're going to be going back through it in approximately five seconds. I have no idea what you're expecting to gain by...' The words died in his throat as the nun removed her hood and hair the colour of a pale moonbeam tumbled in shiny waves over her black habit.

'I'm not a nun, Mr Ziakas.' Her voice was soft, breathy and perfect for the bedroom, a thought that clashed uncomfortably with the vision of her in a nun's outfit.

'Of course you're not,' Stefan drawled, his eyes fixed on her glorious hair, 'but you managed to convince my hardened PA so I suppose you should get points for that.' Suddenly he was annoyed with Maria for allowing herself to be so easily manipulated. 'I'm used to women using all sorts of devices in order to meet me, but I've never yet had one stoop so low as to impersonate a nun. It smacks of desperate behaviour.'

'I'm not impersonating anyone. But it was essential that I keep a low profile.'

'I hate to break this to you, but in the business district of Athens a nun's habit is *not* considered camouflage. You stand out like a penguin in the Sahara. If you want to blend, next time dress in a suit.'

'I couldn't risk being recognised.' Her eyes flickered to the huge glass windows of his office and after a moment she sidled across and peered down at the city while he watched in mounting exasperation.

Who would recognise her? Who was she? Someone's wife?

There *was* something vaguely familiar about her face. His mind coming up blank, he tried to imagine her without her clothes to see if he could place her, but mentally stripping a nun proved a stretch even for him. 'I don't sleep with married women so that can't be the reason for the elaborate subterfuge. Do we know each other? If so, you're going to have to remind me.' He raised an eyebrow as a prompt. 'Where? When? I admit to being hopeless with names.'

She dragged her gaze from the view, those green eyes direct. 'When and where what?'

Stefan, who hated mysteries and considered tact a quality devoid of reward, was blunt. 'Where and when did we have sex? I'm sure it was amazing but you're going to have to remind me of the details.'

She made a sound in her throat. 'I haven't had sex with you!'

'Are you sure?'

Green eyes stared back at him. 'If rumour is correct, Mr Ziakas, sex with you is a memorable experience. Is it something I'm likely to have forgotten?'

More intrigued than he would have been willing to admit, Stefan sat back in his chair. 'You clearly know a great deal more about me than I do about you. Which brings me to the obvious question—what are you doing here?'

'You told me to come and see you in five years. Five years is up. It was up last week, actually. You were kind to me. The only person who was.'

There was a wistful note in her voice that sparked all the alarm bells in his head. Trained to detect vulnerability from a hundred paces so that he could give it a wide berth, Stefan cooled his voice.

'Then this is clearly a case of mistaken identity because I'm never kind to women. I work really hard *not* to be or they start to expect it and the next thing you know they're dropping hints about rings, wedding planners and a house in the country. *Not* my style.'

She smiled at that. 'You were definitely kind to me. Without you I think I would have thrown myself over-board at that party. You talked to me for the whole night. You gave me hope.'

Stefan, all too aware that he was widely regarded as the executioner of women's hopes, raised his eyebrows. He stared at that glorious hair and filed through his memory bank. 'Definitely a case of mistaken identity. If I'd met you, we definitely wouldn't have wasted a night talking. I would have taken you to bed.'

'You told me to come back in five years.'

That news caught his attention and Stefan narrowed his eyes. 'I'm impressed by my own restraint.'

'My father would have killed you.'

*My father would have killed you.*

Stefan stared at her, his eyes sweeping her face for clues, and suddenly he stilled. Those beautiful washed-green eyes were a rare colour he'd only seen once before, hidden behind a pair of unflattering glasses. 'Selene? Selene Antaxos.'

'You *do* recognise me.'

'Barely. *Theé mou*—' His eyes swept her frame. 'You've—grown.' He remembered her as a gangly blonde who still had to grow into her lean body. An awkward teen-ager completely dominated by her overprotective father. A pampered princess never allowed out of her heavily guarded palace.

*Stay away from my daughter, Ziakas.*

It was the unspoken threat that had made him deter-mined to talk to her.

Just thinking of the name Antaxos was enough to ruin his day and now here was the daughter, standing in his office.

Dark emotion rippled through him, unwelcome and un-wanted.

He reminded himself that the daughter wasn't respon-sible for the sins of the father.

'Why are you dressed as a nun?'

'I had to sneak past my father's security.'

'I can't imagine that was easy. Of course if your father didn't make so many enemies he wouldn't need an entire army to protect him.' Blocking the feelings that rose in-side him, he stood up and strolled round his desk. 'What are you doing here?'

The one thing he did remember from that night was feeling sorry for her and the reason he remembered it was because he so rarely felt sorry for anyone. He believed that people made their own choices in life, but he'd taken one look at her in all her leggy, uncomfortable misery and de-cided that being the daughter of Stavros Antaxos must be the shortest straw anyone could ever draw.

'I'll get to that in a minute.' She bent down and caught hold of the hem of her habit. 'Do you mind if I take this off? It's really hot.'

'Where did you get it? The local dressing-up shop?'

'I was educated by the nuns on Poulos, the island next to ours, and they've always been very supportive. They lent it to me but there's no point in keeping it on now I'm safe with you.'

Knowing that most women considered him anything but 'safe', Stefan watched in stunned disbelief as she wriggled and struggled until finally she freed herself and emerged with her hair in tangled disarray. Underneath she was wearing a white silk shirt teamed with a smart black pen-cil skirt that hugged legs designed to turn a man's mind to pulp.

'I almost boiled to death on the ferry. You have no idea. That's why I couldn't wear the jacket.'

'Jacket?'

'The jacket from my suit. It's designed to be worn in an air-conditioned office, not a floating tin can which is how the ferry feels.'

Stefan wrenched his gaze from those bare legs, feeling as if he'd been hit round the head with a brick. Staring into those green eyes, he looked for some sign of the awkward teenage girl he'd met years before. 'You look different.'

'I should hope so. I hope I look like a businesswoman because that's what I am.' She slid her arms into a jacket that matched the skirt, scooped up her hair and pinned it with brisk efficiency. 'When you met me five years ago I had spots and braces. I was hideous.'

*She wasn't hideous now.* 'Does your father know you're here?'

'What do you think?'

The corner of her mouth dimpled into a naughty smile and Stefan stared at that smile, hypnotised by her lips, trying to clear his mind of wicked thoughts.

'I think your father must be having a few sleepless nights.' The wicked thoughts still very much in play, he tried desperately to see her as she'd been that night on the boat. Young and vulnerable. 'I should offer you a drink. Would you like a—' he groped for something suitable '—a glass of milk or something?'

She pushed some loose strands of her hair away from her face in a gesture that somehow managed to be both self-conscious and seductive. 'I'm not six. Do you often offer your visitors milk?'

'No, but I don't usually entertain minors in my office.'

'I'm not a minor. I'm all grown up.'

'Yes. I can see that.' Stefan loosened his collar and discovered it was already undone. He wondered if the air-conditioning in his office was failing. 'So—why don't you tell me why you're here?'

If she wanted him to ruin her father, they might yet find themselves with a common goal.

'I'm here about business, of course. I have a business proposition.'

Huge eyes were fixed hopefully on his face and Stefan felt an instant pull of lust. The explosion of attraction was instant, unmistakable—and entirely inappropriate given the circumstances.

Apart from the obvious physical changes she still looked as innocent as she had that night on the boat. It would be asking for trouble. Even he wasn't going to stoop that low.

'I'm not known for doing favours for people.'

'I know. And I'm not expecting a favour. I know a lot about you. I know you date different women all the time because you don't want a relationship. I know that in business they call you all sorts of things, including ruthless and uncaring.'

'Those are generally good traits to have in business.'

'And you never deny any of those awful things they write about you. You're happy to be portrayed as the big bad wolf.'

'And yet still you're here.'

'I'm not afraid of you. You sat with me for seven hours and talked to me when no one else could be bothered.' Folding the nun's habit carefully, she leaned forward to stuff it into her bag, oblivious to the fact that the movement gave him a perfect view of the curve of her breasts above a hint of lacy bra.

Stefan made a valiant attempt to avert his eyes and failed. 'You were sweet.'

He emphasised the word for his own benefit. If there

was one thing designed to kill his libido it was 'sweet', so why the hell was he painfully aroused? And why was she looking at him with big trusting eyes when what he should have been seeing was an appropriate degree of caution?

*Come into my house, Little Red Riding Hood, and close the door behind you.*

Caution nowhere in sight, she gave him a warm smile. 'It's a bit embarrassing to remember it, to be honest. I was so upset I would have done anything just to make my father mad, but you refused to take advantage of me even though you hate him. You didn't laugh at me when I told you I wanted to set up my own business and you didn't laugh when I flirted with you. You told me to come and find you in five years, which I thought was very tactful.'

She spoke quickly, almost breathless as she got the words out, and Stefan stared at her for a long moment, all his instincts telling him that something wasn't quite right.

Was he seeing desperation or enthusiasm?

Stefan bought himself some time. 'Are you sure you wouldn't like something cold to drink?'

'I'd *love* some champagne.'

'It's ten in the morning.'

'I know. It's just that I've never tasted it and I thought this would be the perfect opportunity. According to the internet you live a champagne lifestyle.' There was a wistful note in her tone that didn't make sense. He'd assumed the Antaxos family bathed in champagne. They were certainly rich enough.

'Believe it or not I try and restrict my champagne consumption until the end of my working day.' Clenching his jaw, Stefan hit a button on his phone. 'Maria? Bring us a jug of water, or lemonade, or—' he racked his brains for a suitable soft drink '—or something soft and refreshing.

With ice,' he added as an afterthought. 'Lots of ice. And some pastries.'

'That's thoughtful of you. I'm starving.'

Stefan leaned against his desk, maintaining a safe distance. 'So—you say you have a business proposition. Tell me about it and I'll tell you if I can help.' Those words felt alien on his tongue. When did he ever help anyone but himself? He'd learned at an early age to take care of himself and he'd been doing it ever since.

'I want to set up my own business just like you did. That night on the yacht, you inspired me. You talked about how you'd done it all yourself and about how great it felt to be independent and not rely on anyone. I want that.' She dug her hand into her bag again and pulled out a file. 'This is my business plan. I've worked hard on it. I think you'll be impressed.'

Stefan, who was rarely impressed by other people's business plans, gingerly took the pink file from her outstretched hand. 'Is there an electronic version?'

'I didn't want to save it on the computer in case my father found it. It's the figures that count, not the presentation.'

So her father knew nothing about it. Perhaps that explained the hint of nerves he detected beneath all that bounce and optimism.

No doubt this was her summer project, designed to fill the long boring hours that came with being an overprotected heiress, and he was the lucky recipient of her endeavours.

Shaking off the feeling that something wasn't quite right about the whole situation, Stefan flipped open the file and scanned the first page. It was surprisingly professional. 'Candles? That's your business idea?'

'Not just candles. Scented candles.' Her voice vibrated

with enthusiasm. 'I went to school in a convent. I started making candles in craft lessons and I experimented with different scents. I have three different ones.'

*Candles*, Stefan thought. The most boring, pointless product on planet earth.

How the hell was he going to let her down gently? He had no experience of letting people down gently. He just dropped them from a great height and stepped over their broken remains.

Clearing his throat, he cultivated what he hoped was an interested expression. 'Why don't you tell me a bit more about what makes them special? Top line? I don't need detail.' Please, God, no detail. As far as he was concerned talking about candles would be one step down from talking about the weather.

'I've called one Relax, one Energise and one—' her cheeks turned a deeper shade of pink '—Seduction.'

Something in the way she hesitated over the word made him glance up from the file. She was trembling with anticipation, and all it took was one glance to know that his first assumption had been correct.

She was a bored heiress, playing at business.

And now she'd prompted him he could clearly remember the night they'd met.

She'd been a teenager—miserable, confused and self-conscious. An ugly duckling dumped in the middle of a flock of elite swans with a doting father who barely took his eyes off her. None of the other men had dared talk to her, none of the women had wanted to, so she'd stood alone, her awkwardness almost painful to witness.

But she was no longer that teenager. She was all woman, and she knew it.

Stavros Antaxos must be having *lots* of sleepless nights.

And now she was looking at him with those big eyes filled with unwavering trust.

Stefan knew she couldn't have found a man less worthy of that trust.

He wondered just how much she knew about his relationship with her father.

The atmosphere in the room shifted.

When he was sure he had his reactions under control, he closed the file slowly and looked at her. 'So your candles are called, Relax, Energise and Seduction?'

'That's right.'

'And just how much,' he asked slowly, 'do you know about seduction?'

# CHAPTER TWO

GREAT. Of all the questions to ask, he had to ask that one.

Not market share or growth forecasts—seduction.

Selene maintained the smile she'd been practising—her business smile—while her brain raced around in crazy circles getting nowhere.

What did she know about seduction? Nothing. Nor was it a skill she was ever likely to need unless her life changed radically. What she did know was that without his help she'd never get her mother away from the island. It was up to her to prove she had a viable business. 'What do I know about seduction? Not a lot. But you know what they say— you don't have to travel the world to teach geography.'

She didn't add that she had her imagination and that was already working overtime.

She'd often wondered if her teenage brain had exaggerated his appeal or whether her own misery that night, together with his kindness, had somehow mingled together to create a god from a man. But he was as gorgeous as she remembered—power, strength and raw virility merged together in a muscle-packed masculine frame that made her feel dizzy with thoughts she couldn't seem to control.

Physically he was imposing, but it wasn't his impressive height or the width of those shoulders that shook her. It was something less easily defined. A hint of danger—

the sense that underneath that beautifully cut suit and the external trappings of success lurked a man who wielded more power than even her father.

Flustered, Selene tried to remember the way he'd been on that night five years earlier, but it was almost impossible to equate that kind stranger with this cool, sophisticated businessman standing in front of her.

And the fact that he was flicking through her amateurish document so quickly left her squirming with embarrassment. He barely took any time as he glanced at each page, nothing in his face giving a hint as to his thoughts. Clearly he thought it was rubbish.

Her mother was right. He was never going to help her.

He was right at the top of his game, a busy man with huge demands on his time. According to her research, thousands of people approached his company every year for business advice and he helped less than a handful of people.

While she waited for him to comment she sipped the lemonade but after a couple of minutes of squirming in her seat restraint left her. 'So tell me honestly—' *Is it a crappy idea?* God, no, she couldn't say that. 'Er—do you see this as an investment opportunity?' She felt like such a fraud. A total impostor, just waiting for him to laugh her out of his office. It must have been obvious to him that she'd never had a business meeting with anyone except her own reflection.

He closed the file, then turned to put it on his desk. His tailored shirt pulled across his wide shoulders, emphasising hard muscle, and her heart started to thud.

She dreamed about him all the time. Had thought about him almost every hour since that night.

'Selene?'

His voice was gentle and she looked at him, startled and embarrassed to have let her concentration lapse.

'Yes. I'm listening.'

The look in his eyes told her he was skilled at reading minds and hers was probably the easiest he'd ever read.

Suddenly her mouth felt as if she hadn't touched liquid for a week.

If he guessed how she felt about him she'd die on the spot.

Her trawl of the internet had revealed a lot about his relationship with women and every scandalous story had made her heart beat just a little bit faster because they spoke of a life so far removed from hers that it was like listening to a fairy story. Glittering parties. Opening nights. Opera. Ballet. Film premieres. The list was endless, as were the names of the beautiful women he'd paraded on his arm at one time or another, and it was all she could think about now as she stared at him, waiting for his answer.

'These candles—do you have a sample?'

'Yes.' She fumbled in her bag, trying to ignore the nerves fluttering low in her belly. It was as if just being in the same room as him had somehow triggered all the alarms in her body. The attraction was so shockingly powerful it knocked her off-balance. She definitely needed to get out more. This was what happened when a father locked a daughter away. She'd turned into a raging nymphomaniac. Stefan Ziakas was going to be lucky to escape with his clothes still on.

Disconcerted, she glanced at him but that turned out to be a bigger mistake. Thick, inky lashes highlighted eyes of molten gold and his mouth was a slim, sensual line in a face sculpted by the devil to tempt women to the dark side.

Selene was unsettled by just how desperately she wanted to be taken to the dark side.

'I know this business idea has potential.' She was brisk and businesslike and hoped he wouldn't guess that she'd practised this a hundred times in the mirror. 'I have some packaging samples, but they might need to be adapted. We live in a fast-paced, stressful world. Scented candles are an affordable luxury and I'm not the only one who thinks so. The market is currently growing at forty percent.'

His mouth was such a perfect shape, she thought. She'd noticed the same thing that night on the boat as she'd stared and stared at him, willing him to kiss her. There had been a few breathless moments when she'd thought he might do just that but he hadn't, so clearly it had just been wishful thinking on her part.

Leaning forward, he extracted the candle from her grip and turned it in his fingers. 'You're expecting me to believe that this is the next big thing?'

'Why not? Don't you like candles?'

A smile played around that sexy mouth. 'You want an honest answer?'

She remembered that this was a business meeting. That she was a businesswoman. 'Yes,' she said firmly. 'Yes, I do.'

'I'm a man. The only reason a man is ever going to like candles is if there is a power cut and the generator fails, or if he finds himself dining with a woman who is ugly.'

And she was willing to bet he never found himself in that position. 'But candles are about so much more than romantic lighting in a restaurant.' She tried not to think about him dining with a beautiful woman. 'The one I've named Seduction is scented with lotus blossom and it creates the perfect atmosphere for—for—'

'For?'

His eyes gleamed and she had a strong suspicion he

was laughing at her. 'Seduction,' she said lamely, suddenly
wishing she'd called it something else.

'And you know that because…?'

His voice was disturbingly soft and the laughter had
gone from his eyes. Now his gaze was intense—*serious*—
and Selene felt as if she'd been seared by the flame of a
blowtorch.

'Because people have told me that's the case.'

'But you've never tried it yourself.' It was a statement,
not a question, and she felt her face burn along with her
body.

She wished he'd stuck to a conversation about market
share and forecasts. 'I've tried Relax and Energise.'

'So no market research on Seduction?'

'Yes, just not—personal research.'

There was a long, pulsing silence and then he put the
candle down and leaned his hips on the desk, the movement of his trousers revealing expensive polished shoes.
'Let me tell you something about seduction, Selene.' His
voice was more seductive than a thousand scented candles. 'To you it's just a word, but it's so much more than
that. Seduction is about tempting, enticing and persuading
until you've driven someone mad with need. Yes, scent is
important, but not the artificial scent of a candle—it's the
individual scent of the person you're with, and it's not just
scent but scent combined with touch and sound.'

Selene couldn't breathe. 'Sound?'

'When I'm with a woman I want to hear the sounds she
makes. I want to hear her pleasure as well as feel it under
my lips and fingers. And then there's taste…' His voice
was softer now, those dangerous eyes velvety dark as he
held her gaze, 'I want to taste every part of her and en-
courage her to taste every part of me.'

'Y-you do?'

'Scent, touch, hearing, sound, taste—seduction uses all the senses, not just one. It's about taking over someone's mind and body until they're no longer capable of rational thought—until they want just one thing and one thing only—until they're reduced to an elemental state where nothing matters but the moment.'

Selene felt dizzy. 'I think I might need to rename my candle.'

'I'm sure there are men out there who would be only too happy to use a scented candle as a prop. I'm just not one of them.'

He wouldn't need any external props to seduce a woman. Those hands would be sure and skilled. And as for his mouth—

Realising her own hands were shaking, she tucked them firmly into her lap. 'Just because you're not my target audience, it doesn't mean I don't have a viable product.' Proud of that response, she carried on. 'Will you teach me what I need to know?' As his brows rose she continued, flustered. 'I mean about marketing. Running a business.'

'I have a question.'

'Yes, of course you do. Ask me anything.' He was so cool and sophisticated and she was no more interesting than her seventeen-year-old self. 'You want to know more about the product? It's a really good-quality candle. It's made of beeswax and it's smokeless and virtually drip-free.'

'I can hardly contain my excitement.' But he was smiling as he picked up the candle again and she had a feeling his mind was still on seduction rather than the product in his hand. 'That wasn't my question.'

'Oh. I expect you want to ask me about my revenue projections. I've had an order for five thousand from Hot Spa. They're the most exclusive chain of spa hotels in

Greece. But of course you know that...' Her voice tailed off. 'You own them.'

Stefan handed the candle back to her. 'That wasn't my question, either.'

She gulped. Licked her lips. 'Sorry—I'm talking too much. I do that when I'm—' *desperate* '—excited.'

'My first question,' he said slowly, 'is why someone like you would even want to set up a business. Are you bored?'

Bored? She bit back a bubble of hysterical laughter. 'No.'

'You're an heiress. You don't need to run a business.'

*He had no idea.* 'I want to prove myself.'

He stared at her for a long moment. 'Which brings me to my second question—why come to me? If you're serious about this then your father could put up the investment.'

Selene made sure her smile didn't slip. 'I don't want my father's name on it. This is my project. I want to own it. I don't want anyone doing me favours.' It was a lie, of course. She needed all the favours she could grab. 'I can't approach the banks because they won't help me without asking my father's permission. I tried to think of someone who isn't under his thumb and I came up with you. You told me to look you up in five years—'

The silence stretched between them.

Looking at his hard, handsome face she felt the confidence drain out of her. In an appalling flash of clarity she realised she'd made a monumental mistake. Losing her nerve, horribly embarrassed, she rose to her feet. 'Thank you for listening.'

He stirred, uncrossed those long, lean legs and stood up, dominating the room. 'You came to me for a business loan. Don't you want to hear my answer?'

'I—I thought you might need time to think about it.'

'I've had all the time I need.'

So the answer was no. Her shoulders sagged. Misery seeped into her veins.

'Right. Well—'

'My answer is yes.'

Because it wasn't what she was expecting to hear, it took a moment for his words to sink in.

'Seriously? You're not just saying that because I've made it hard for you to say no?'

'No is my favourite word. I don't find it hard to say.'

*But he wasn't saying it to her.* 'I just thought you might be agreeing to help me because you don't want me to feel bad.'

A strange expression crossed his face. 'That isn't the reason.'

His eyes were on her mouth and she saw something in his face that made her heart pound just a little harder in her chest.

*I lie awake at night thinking about you.*

He was silent for a long moment and then strolled to the window and stared across the city. 'It is going to drive your father crazy. Does that bother you?'

Yes, it bothered her. Her safety and the safety of her mother rested on a knife-edge, which was why she had to get away.

She had a sudden urge to tell him the truth, but years of keeping her secret and loyalty to her mother prevented her from doing it. And she knew enough about Stefan Ziakas to know that he wasn't going to be interested in the details of her personal life. He avoided all that, didn't he? He would never let anything personal interfere with business. 'He has to understand that this is my life and I want to make my own mistakes. I want to be independent.'

'So this is delayed teenage rebellion?'

Let him think that if he wanted to. 'I know you're not

afraid of going up against him. I read that article recently—
the headline was "Clash of the Titans". And the mere mention of your name is enough to put my father in a bad
mood for days.' She stared at his broad shoulders, wondering if the sudden tension she saw there was a product
of her imagination.

'And has he ever told you why?'

'Of course not. My father would never discuss business
with a woman. He won't be pleased with me but he'll have
to get used to the idea.' The ache in her arm reminded her
just how displeased he was likely to be. 'I hadn't thought
about the implications for you. If it bothers you that he'll
be angry...'

'That's not a problem for me.' There was the briefest
pause and then he turned back to his desk in a smooth,
confident movement and pressed a button on the phone.
Without any further discussion or questions he instructed
someone in his legal department to start making all the
necessary arrangements to loan her whatever money she
needed.

Having braced herself for rejection, or at least a load of
awkward questions, Selene stared at him, unable to believe
what she was hearing.

He was going to lend her the money. Just like that.

It couldn't be this easy, could it? Nothing in life was
this easy.

The knot of tension that had been lodged in her stomach
for as long as she could remember started to ease. Anxiety was replaced by a rush of euphoria that made her feel
like dancing round the room.

Apparently unaware of the impact of his decision,
Stefan ended the phone call, supremely relaxed. 'It's done.
My only stipulation is that you work with one of my busi-
ness development managers who will give you access to

all the in-house resources of the Ziakas Corporation. That way you won't be ripped off by suppliers or customers, and basically you can draw on whatever funds you need.'

He was watching her from under those thick, dark lashes and her stomach flipped.

He was *gorgeous.*

People had him *so* wrong. It wasn't right that everyone should talk about him in hushed voices as some sort of cold, conscienceless machine when he was obviously capable of all the normal human emotions. Maybe he was hard and ruthless in some aspects of his life, but to her he'd been nothing but kind.

'I—' She was dizzy with euphoria, hardly able to get her head around what had just happened. She was going to be able to start her own business, rent a small apartment and help her mother leave her father. She wanted to fling her arms round him and then remembered that this was a business meeting and she was pretty sure people didn't do things like that in business meetings. 'That's an excellent outcome. Thank you. You won't be sorry.' She should shake his hand. Yes, that was what she should do. Shake his hand to seal the deal.

Standing up, she walked towards him and held out her hand.

His hand closed over hers, warm and strong, and suddenly what had begun as a simple handshake became something else entirely. He smelt good. She had no idea whether it was shampoo or something different but it made her want to bury her face in his neck and inhale deeply. All she had to do was lean forward and she'd be kissing him. Horrified by how tempted she was, she looked down at her hand instead and saw the expensive watch on his wrist and his lean, bronzed fingers linked intimately with hers.

Her stomach clenched.

Power and masculinity throbbed from him and suddenly all she could think about was sex—which was crazy because she knew nothing about sex.

*But he did.*

'So now that's out of the way,' he drawled softly, 'the question is how far are you willing to take this quest for independence?'

Busy imagining those strong, confident hands on her body, she felt her heart thud. 'Why are you asking?'

'Because I'm hosting a party tonight and I find myself minus a date. How do you feel about celebrating your new-found independence in style?'

Her eyes lifted to his and she saw amusement there. Amusement and something a little bit dangerous.

The excitement came in a whoosh that drove the air from her lungs.

Her head spun. The hungry look in his eyes was interfering with the normally smooth rhythm of her breathing. 'You're inviting me to a party?' She never went to parties unless her father decided it was time to play Happy Families in public. They were the most painful moments of her life. And the loneliest, all of them fake.

She'd never been to a party for the sheer fun of it. Never been to a party where she was allowed to be herself.

She wondered why he was asking her.

'If I say no does that mean—?'

'You have my agreement on the loan. Your answer has no effect on our deal.'

In that case she should walk away. There would be time to party once she was safely away from the island. Selene licked her lips. 'What sort of party is it?'

'A strictly grown-up event. No jelly or ice cream in sight.'

A party. *With him.*

'You're asking me to come as your date?'

'That's right.'

The excitement was sharper than when he'd agreed to lend her the money. A date. A party. With this man. She'd never done anything like that in her life.

She should say no. Now that he'd agreed to help her she should get back to Antaxos, persuade her mother to leave and be long gone before her father returned. She couldn't possibly say yes even though she wanted to more than she'd ever wanted anything in her life.

On the other hand, why not?

For the first time in her life she was free to make her own decision about something. For once her father wasn't dictating her actions, no one was watching her and her mother was safe. She had no one to think about but herself. If she wanted to go to a party, she could. And wasn't that the point of all this? To be able to live her life the way she wanted to live it?

Feeling liberated, she opened her mouth. 'I don't have anything to wear.'

'That's easily solved.'

'I have this fantasy about wearing a wicked red dress and drinking champagne from a tall, slim glass with a handsome man in a dinner jacket. Would we drink champagne?'

His mouth curved into a smile so sexy it should have been illegal. 'All night.'

'And would we—?'

The devil danced in his eyes and his mouth moved fractionally closer to hers. 'If you're asking what I think you're asking then the answer is yes, we definitely would.'

# CHAPTER THREE

'How did he arrange for these dresses to be delivered so fast? And how did he guess my size? On second thoughts, don't answer that.' Confronted with a rail of the most beautiful dresses she'd ever seen, Selene felt as if she'd stepped onto a Hollywood movie set. Part of her felt anxious about her decision to stay, but another part felt wildly excited. She listened to the excited part and ignored the anxiety. That, she reasoned, came from too many years of not being allowed to make her own decisions. It was natural that it felt strange.

Maria pulled an elegant clutch bag from tissue paper. 'When Stefan picks up the phone, people respond at supersonic speed. The benefits of being a man of power.'

'Except that you were the one who did the phoning.'

'True.' Maria smiled. 'Power by proxy. Why don't you start by choosing a dress?'

'Is Stefan joining us?'

'He sends his apologies. He has one more important meeting he has to take before you leave.'

'I don't mind. I'd be too self-conscious to strip in front of him anyway and it's more fun with a woman. It was thoughtful of him to arrange for you to help me.' She saw Maria's expression change. 'You don't think he's thoughtful?'

The other woman removed a beautiful pair of shoes from a bag. 'That's certainly an adjective I've not heard applied to him before.'

'He's running a business. Of course he has to be tough. But on the two occasions I've met him he's been kind to me.'

Maria put the shoes down in front of her. 'You have no idea how pleased I am to hear that. Why don't you pick a dress and try it on? Because once he's finished his meeting he won't want to hang around. Is there anything in particular that grabs your attention?'

'The red one.' There was no other choice for her and the colour matched her mood. *Bold.* 'I've never worn anything like that in my life.' She reached for a shimmering sheath of scarlet with jewels on the strapless bodice. 'This is *gorgeous.* Will it be over the top?'

'No. It's a very glamorous party. That dress is very sophisticated.' Maria stared at it for a long moment. 'Are you sure you don't want to pick a different one? Maybe the blue?'

'You don't think Stefan will like the red one?'

'I think he might like it a little too much.'

'How can he possibly like it too much?'

'Selene...' The other woman hesitated. 'Are you sure you want to go to this party?'

'*Want* to go? I'm *desperate* to go. You have no idea how boring my life has been up to now. I'm going to dress up, drink champagne and have the most amazing night with Stefan.'

'Just as long as you know that's all it will be.' Maria cleared her throat gently. 'Stefan is the stuff of female dreams, but he quickly turns into a nightmare for most women. He isn't the happy-ever-after type—you do know that, don't you? Because you seem like a really nice girl and I'd hate to see you hurt.'

Selene paused with her hand on the dress.

*She knew all about hurt and this wasn't it.* 'I won't be hurt. I'm excited. It will be fun to just enjoy myself for one night.' Fun to be able to make a decision to go to a party. Fun to decide what to wear. For once, her life felt almost normal.

'You don't usually enjoy yourself?'

'I have an overprotective father.' Realising that she'd said more than she intended to, Selene draped the dress over her arm. 'Is there somewhere I can try it on?'

'You'll need underwear.' Maria handed her several boxes. 'Go and change and if you need help, call me.'

An hour later Selene was the proud owner of the most beautiful dress she'd ever seen, along with a small emergency wardrobe suitable for an overnight stay at a luxury villa on a Greek island. Ahead of her lay the most exciting night of her life, and if lurking underneath her happiness was a fear that her father might return early she dismissed it.

That wasn't going to happen.

She'd have plenty of time to get home, persuade her mother to leave and be long gone before he returned.

'You can't do this. You can't take that girl to the party. It's immoral.'

Stefan glanced up from the papers he was signing to find Maria standing in front of his desk like a general facing down an enemy army.

'Now, *that's* the look you're supposed to give unwanted visitors.' He flung down his pen. 'Do I need to remind you that *you* were the one who showed her into the lion's den?'

'I'm serious, Stefan. Take someone else. Someone more your type.'

'Just this morning you were lecturing me on picking the wrong type. Make up your mind.'

'I wasn't telling you to prey on innocent girls.'

'She's an adult. She knows what she's doing.' He picked up his pen and flicked through the papers on his desk.

'She's an idealist. She thinks you're thoughtful and kind.'

'I know.' Smiling, Stefan signed the back page. 'For once, I'm the good guy. An unfamiliar role, I admit, but I'm surprised by how much I'm enjoying the novelty.'

'You're treating her like a shiny new toy that you can play with.' Maria's mouth set in a firm line. 'Send her home to her father.'

Stefan was careful not to let the sudden flare of emotion show on his face. Slowly, he put his pen down. 'Do you know who her father is?'

'No. Although she mentioned something about him being overprotective.'

'Is that a useful synonym for "tyrant", I wonder? Her father, Maria, is Stavros Antaxos.' He watched as Maria's face lost some of its colour. 'Yes. Exactly.' He heard his voice harden and it irritated him that just saying the name was enough to do that to him. He'd had over two decades to learn how to control his response.

'How on earth can a man like that produce someone as charming as Selene?'

He'd been asking himself the same question.

'I assume she takes after her mother.'

Maria looked troubled. 'But why would someone as wealthy as her, from such a close family, come to you?'

He'd been asking himself the same question. Repeatedly. 'I'm a hero, didn't you know? I'm the first man women think of when they're in trouble.'

'You're the man who causes the trouble.'

'Ouch, that's harsh.' Stefan leaned back and stretched out his legs. 'Here I am, sword at the ready, eager to chop the head off a dragon to save the maiden, and all you can do is knock my confidence.'

She didn't smile. 'Is that really what's going on here? Because it occurred to me that maybe you're using the maiden to taunt the dragon.'

Stefan's smile didn't slip. 'When we were dishing out roles in this company I picked cynic, not you.'

'We're all cynical here. It's contagious. Does she know how much her father hates you? Does she know the story?'

No one knew the story. Not even Maria, whom he allowed more liberties than most. Oh, she *thought* she knew—thought it was all about business rivalry and two alpha males acting out their deeply competitive natures. She had no idea how far back it went, or how deep the scars. And why would she? They weren't visible. He didn't allow them to be visible.

'It's because of my relationship with her father that she chose me.'

Maria's mouth flattened with disapproval.

'Are you sure this isn't a case of out of the frying pan and into the fire?'

'You're suggesting I'm worse than Antaxos? That is hardly a complimentary view of one's boss.'

'We're not talking about work right now. My admiration for your intellect and business skills is boundless but when it comes to women you're bad news. What are your plans for her, Stefan?'

'When it comes to women I never make plans. You should know that by now. "Plan" implies a future and we both know I don't think like that. I've agreed to help her with her business—which, by the way, looks remarkably interesting on paper, particularly when you consider the product. And I'm taking her to a party. I intend to provide more fun than she's had in the rest of her life. She can make her own decisions about how she spends her time. She's twenty-two and on a quest for independence.' Stefan battled a disturbingly vivid image of her breasts revealed through a cloud of lace. 'All grown up.'

'She's very inexperienced.'

'Yes. I'm finding that unusually appealing.'

'And does that appeal have anything to do with the fact you are the *last* man her father would want her to be with? Thinking of her with you will drive him demented.'

Stefan smiled. 'I consider that an added bonus.'

'I'm worried about her, Stefan.'

'She came to me. She asked for my help. I'm giving it.' It was obvious that there was something going on beneath the surface and it intrigued him. She was playing a game, but he wasn't sure which game. 'I don't recall you ever being this protective of the women I date before.'

'That's because you normally date women who don't need protecting from anything.'

'So maybe it's time for a change.' Cutting off the conversation, he rose to his feet. 'How long until she's ready? No doubt she's still pulling clothes on and off, trying to decide what to wear.'

'She decided what to wear in less than five seconds and it took her barely more than that to try it on.'

Used to women who could waste the best part of a day selecting one outfit, he was impressed. 'I like her more and more.'

'She has a very high opinion of you.'

'I know.' He walked past her to the door and Maria made a frustrated sound.

'Where is your conscience?'

Stefan picked up his jacket. 'I don't have a conscience.'

When he'd mentioned his villa she'd imagined somewhere small. She hadn't for one moment expected this spacious, airy mansion with high ceilings and acres of glass. Here, in this testament to innovative architecture, there were no dark corners or contagious gloom, just dazzling light exploding across marble floors and picking out the warm Mediterranean colours that turned the deceptively simple interior into a luxurious sanctuary.

Outside, a vine-shaded terrace led to gardens that created a blur of extravagant colour as they tumbled down a gentle slope that led to a crescent beach. And even there the idyll didn't end. Unlike Antaxos, there were no killer rocks or dark, fathomless depths that threatened to swallow a person and leave no trace. Just sand of the softest, creamiest yellow and tiny silver fish dancing in the clear shallow water. The whole scene was so tempting that she, who avoided water, just wanted to rip off her shoes and plunge into the safe, cool shallows.

'So this is why people see the Greek Islands as a tourist destination.' She spoke without thinking and her unguarded comment earned her a questioning look.

'Was the reason for that choice in doubt?'

Staring out of huge windows across the garden to the turquoise sea, she felt something stir inside her. It was like living a life in black and white and suddenly seeing it in colour. 'Antaxos isn't anything like this. No soft sand, just nasty rocks—' She just stopped herself mentioning the rumour that a woman who'd been madly in love with her father had once fallen from those rocks and drowned.

'My father's house—our house—is built of stone with small windows.' She managed to say it without shuddering. 'The design supposedly keeps the heat out.' And it kept everything and everyone else out, too. The bleak, dark atmosphere inside the place had somehow permeated the stone so that even the building felt unfriendly. 'It's stuffy in the summer and dark and cheerless in the winter. I like the light here. You have a very happy home.'

'Happy?' He glanced up at the villa, a faint frown between his eyes. 'You think a building has moods?'

'Definitely. Don't you?'

'I think a building is a building.'

'Oh, no, that isn't true. A building can make a person feel different. Here, the sunshine makes you want to smile. And all this *space*—it feels like being free.' She spread her arms. 'I've always wanted to be a bird so I can fly.' *Fly away from the island that had held her trapped for so long.*

But she'd finally escaped. She'd done it.

This was the start of her new life.

Excited, she did a twirl. Stefan shot out a hand and steadied her before she lost her balance. 'Probably best if you don't fly here. I've seen pictures of your home on Antaxos. You live in a building the size of a castle.'

Selene was conscious of the strength of his fingers on her arm. 'It isn't anything like this. My father doesn't like spending money on material things.'

'Is there anything that your father *does* like?'

*Hurting people.*

She stood, searching for an appropriate response to his question, her heart a ball of pain in her chest. 'Winning,' she said finally. 'He likes winning.'

'Yes.' His hand dropped abruptly from her arm. 'Yes, he does.'

And he'd know, of course, because he was her father's

biggest business rival. She sensed the anger in him and she also sensed something more. Something dark lurked behind those sexy eyes. 'You really hate my father, don't you?'

'It's true to say he's not my favourite person in the world.' The deceptively light banter and that attractive slanting smile didn't fool her.

This man was every bit as tough as her father.

She felt a twinge of unease, but already he was strolling ahead of her. She tried to ignore the little voice in her head telling her this might not have been such a good idea after all.

It was her first party. Her first 'date' with a man. It was natural to be a little apprehensive.

She followed him through a beautiful living space with white walls and uninterrupted views of the sea into the most beautiful bedroom she'd ever seen.

Forgetting her unease, Selene stared around her in delight. 'It's gorgeous. There's a pool outside the doors and you can see the sea from the bed. It's stunning. Is this my room?'

He turned to her with a slow, deliberate smile. 'It's *my* room,' he said, his tone soft and intimate as he lifted his hand and gently pushed a strand of hair out of her eyes, 'but you're sharing it, *koukla mou.*'

She didn't know whether it was the endearment that made her heart bump harder, the seductive brush of his fingers against her cheek or the anticipation of what was to come. 'The bed looks comfortable.'

'It is. Unfortunately proving that will have to wait until later.'

'I didn't mean that.'

'I know. I'm finding your tendency to speak before you think surprisingly endearing.'

The crazy thing was she wasn't normally like that. At home she had to guard every word. She wondered why she'd suddenly lost that built-in inhibition and decided it was just because her father wasn't present. It was liberating not to have to watch what she said. 'I'm going to zip my mouth.'

That dark gaze dropped to her mouth. 'Don't. I like it.'

Heart thudding, she looked at his lips. Noticed that they were firm and slightly curved.

'No,' he said gently.

Her eyes lifted to his. 'No?'

'No, I'm not going to kiss you. At least, not yet. Tempted though I am to snatch a few moments, there are some things that shouldn't be rushed and your first time is one of them.'

The fact that he knew it was her first time should have embarrassed her but it didn't, and she didn't waste time denying something that would be obvious to a man like him.

There was an almost electric connection between them that she felt right through her body. Warmth spread through her pelvis and she felt shaky with need. She wanted him to kiss her so badly she couldn't imagine how she was going to last a whole evening without just grabbing him. 'Maybe I don't mind being rushed.'

Frowning slightly, he brushed this thumb over her lower lip, the movement slow and lingering. 'You need to be more cautious around men.'

And normally she *was* cautious, of course, not least because all the men she knew worked for her father in some capacity. But Stefan was different. He wasn't afraid of her father. And he'd got her through that horrible night when she was a teenager. 'I don't feel a need to be cautious around you. Does that sound crazy?'

'Yes.'

'I trust you.'

'Don't.'

'Why not? You're not being paid by my father.'

Silence stretched between them.

His eyes glittering, he lowered his head a fraction until his forehead was against hers and their mouths were a breath apart. The brush of his fingers against her cheek was gentle and seductive at the same time. 'You've come here with me but I want you to know it's not too late for you to change your mind.'

'I'm not going to change my mind.'

His gaze darkened. 'Maybe I should just cancel the party and we can have our own party here, just the two of us.'

Awareness twisted in her stomach. The tension was stifling. She felt as if she were standing on the edge of a deep, dark pool about to jump, with no idea whether she'd be able to save herself from drowning. 'If we have our own party here, I couldn't wear my new dress.'

'You could wear it for me.' His mouth slanted into that sexy smile. 'And I could remove it.'

Her hand was resting on his arm and she could feel the hardness of his biceps under her fingers. 'Isn't that rather a waste of an expensive dress?'

'The dress is just packaging. It's the product underneath that interests me.' His fingers stroked her neck gently and then his phone rang. He stepped back with a regretful smile. 'Probably a good thing. I need enough time to do justice to the moment. Our guests will be arriving in a few hours and in true Cinderella style *you* need to get ready.'

A few *hours*? 'How long do you think it will take me?'

'In my experience most women take a lifetime to get ready. In the hope of speeding up that process, I've arranged for you to have some help. Not only am I a knight in shining armour, I'm also a fairy godmother. In fact the extent of my benevolence is starting to astonish me.' His phone continued to ring and he dragged it out of his pocket. 'Excuse me. I need to take this.'

As the door closed behind him Selene stood still. Her cheek tingled from the touch of his fingers and the only thing in her head was the memory of hard, male muscle under her fingers.

With a shiver, she wrapped her arms around herself and turned to look at the bed. It was enormous, draped in white linen and facing the sea. Indulgent, luxurious and like nothing she'd ever seen before. Experimenting, she slid off her shoes and jumped into the middle of it, moaning with delight as she felt the soft mound of pillows give beneath her. It was like being hugged by a cloud.

She rolled onto her back and stared up at the ceiling, smiling.

She felt free.

Right this moment no one knew where she was. No one was watching her. No one was reporting her every move to her father. No one had told her where she had to be. She was here because *she* had decided she wanted to be here.

Going to Stefan for help had been her first good decision and agreeing to come to the party had been her second.

Feeling light-headed, she sprang off the bed and explored the rest of the bedroom suite.

There was a ridiculously luxurious bathroom with a wall of glass that made it possible to lie in the bath and look at the sea.

Determined to indulge herself, Selene unpacked her own candles and soap. Then she ran herself a deep bath and lay in it, enjoying the scent of the candle.

She wasn't so naïve she didn't know what was going to

happen and she wanted it to happen. She'd dreamed about Stefan for years. Had had years to think about it. *Imagine it.* It was perfect that he should be the first.

*Soon*, she thought. *Soon she'd know everything there was to know about seduction.*

She washed her hair and was wrapped in a soft towel, wondering why getting ready was supposed to take hours, when there was a tap on the door and two young women entered, clutching several cases.

'Selene? I'm Dana. I'm a genius with hair.' Dana pushed the door shut with the toe of her shoe. 'This is Helena—she's the make-up fairy.'

'I don't own make-up.' It was embarrassing to admit it but her father had never allowed make-up or anything that he described as 'vanity'. He'd only paid for her to have a brace because the dentist had told him it would cost him more in the long run if she didn't have one.

Dana flipped open her case. 'No problem. We have everything you'll need.'

'Do you think you can do something about my freckles and my non-existent eyelashes?'

'You're kidding, right?' Helena peered at her. 'Your eyelashes are incredible. Thick and long. What's wrong with them?'

Selene had assumed it was obvious. 'Don't you think I look a bit freakish? They're so fair they barely show up.'

'Freakish? No, I don't think you look freakish. As for being fair—that's why mascara was invented, sweetie.' With a dazzling smile, she flipped open another case to reveal an array of different make-up. 'I have everything we'll need right here.'

'Hair first.' Dana pulled a chair into the middle of the room. 'Sit. And don't look in the mirror or you'll ruin the "wow" moment and that's our favourite part. Just trust me.'

'Will I recognise myself?'

'You'll be the best version of you.'

Selene, intrigued by what the best version of herself was going to look like, sat still as the girl trimmed her hair, trying not to flinch as blonde curls floated onto her lap. 'You're cutting it short?'

'All I'm doing is taking off the ends to improve the condition and cutting in a few layers to soften it. Stefan threatened never to use me again if I ruin your beautiful hair, although if you want my personal opinion—' Dana squinted at her '—I think it would suit you short.'

He liked her hair. The thought went round and round in her head.

*He liked her hair.*

It was her first compliment—not actually spoken, of course, but a compliment none the less—and with it came the discovery that the feeling of flying was something that could happen inside you. Her spirits lifted and a smile touched her lips, and as well as the smile and the happiness there was something else. A lump in her throat that caught her by surprise.

'It's in great condition.' Dana's fingers moved through her hair as she snipped and combed.

*He liked her hair.*

The girl worked speedily and skilfully, dodging Helena, who was doing Selene's nails.

Once Selene's hair was dry Dana swept it up, twisted and pinned until finally she was satisfied. 'You're ready for make-up.'

'Can your magic make-up box get rid of my freckles?'

'Why would you want to? They're charming. Part of you. We want to keep you looking like you. That's one thing he insisted on. This is just primer I'm using, by the way.' Helena smoothed her fingers over Selene's face. 'You

have beautiful skin.' The girl opened a series of pots, po-
tions, colours, concealers, the sight of which made Selene's
head spin. 'What cleanser do you use?'

'Soap I make myself.' Selene delved into her bag and
pulled out a bar. 'Try it. I make candles, too, but Stefan
isn't convinced there's a market for those.'

'He's a man. What does he know?'

Selene smiled and her heart pounded because finally,
finally, she believed this might actually happen. Her new
life was almost visible, shining like a star in the distance.

The girl sniffed the soap. Her brows rose. 'Smells good.
And your skin is wonderful so that's a good advert.' She
dropped it into her bag. 'I'll try it, thanks.' She turned
back to Selene. 'I'm not going to use too much make-up
on you because you have a wonderfully fresh look and I
don't want to spoil that.'

It took ages, and Selene was just starting to fidget and
wonder how much longer it was going to take when Helena stepped back.

'God, I'm good at my job. You look spectacular. Don't
look in the mirror yet. Get dressed first so that you can
see the full effect all at once.' She grinned. 'I almost feel
sorry for Stefan.'

# CHAPTER FOUR

STEFAN moved slowly among his guests, stirring up expectation.

'So who is she, Stefan?' A Hollywood actress who had been flirting with him for months didn't hide her annoyance at his hints that he'd brought a special guest. 'Not Sonya, I assume?'

'Not Sonya.'

'Why so mysterious? And why is she still in the bedroom and not out here, or is that a question one shouldn't ask?'

'Worn out from too much sex,' someone murmured. Stefan simply smiled and accepted a glass of champagne from one of his hovering staff.

'She leads a very quiet, very private life and this is all very new to her.' He'd discovered early in life that it was best to sail as close to the truth as possible and he stuck to that now as he carefully conjured suspense and interest among his guests.

Carys Bergen, a model who had been flirting with him for several months, strolled up to him. 'You're a wicked man. Who is this reclusive woman that you're about to produce like a rabbit from a magician's hat?'

He left his guests simmering in an atmosphere of expectation and strolled through the villa to the master bedroom suite, scooping another glass of champagne on the way.

At first he thought she wasn't in the room and he gave an impatient frown and glanced around him. 'Selene?'

'I'm here.'

He turned his head.

There was no sign of the awkward schoolgirl. The person standing in front of him in a sheath of shimmering scarlet was all woman.

'That dress was designed for the express purpose of tempting some poor defenceless man to rip it off.' His eyes weren't on the dress, but on the delicious curve of her narrow waist and the swell of her breasts above the tight jewelled bodice.

She smiled, clearly delighted by the effect she was having on him. '"Defenceless" is not a word anyone would use to describe you. And I know you spend your life escorting women who wear stunning dresses so what makes this one special?'

'The person wearing it.'

'Oh, *smooth*, Mr Ziakas.'

Unused to women whose response to compliments was laughter, Stefan handed her a glass. 'Champagne in a tall, slim glass, a red dress and a guy in a dinner jacket. This could be the first time in my life I've made a woman's dreams come true.'

'Mmm, thank you.' She took a mouthful of champagne, her eyes closing as if she wanted to savour the moment. 'It tastes like celebration.' Immediately she took another sip, and then another larger gulp.

Stefan raised his brows. 'If you want to remember the evening, drink slowly.'

'It tastes delicious. I love the feel of the bubbles on my tongue. And one of the best things about my new independence is being able to decide what I drink and what I don't drink.'

'That's fine. But, delighted though I am that you're clearly capable of enjoying the sensual potential of champagne, I'd rather my date wasn't unconscious. From now on take tiny sips and count to a hundred in between.' He held out his arm and she immediately put her empty glass down, took his arm and smiled up at him.

'Thank you.'

That wide, genuine smile knocked him off-balance. He was used to coy, flirtatious and manipulative. 'Friendly' was new to him and he had no idea how to respond.

She appeared to have no sense of caution. No layers of protection between her and the world. How the hell was she going to manage when she was no longer protected by her father's security machine?

'What are you thanking me for?'

'For agreeing to help me, for inviting me to this party and for arranging all these wonderful clothes. It's the perfect way to start my new life. You're my hero.' She stood back slightly, her eyes on his shoulders. 'You look smoking hot in a dinner jacket, by the way. Very macho. I bet all the dragons in Greece are trembling in their caves, or wherever it is dragons live when they're not munching on innocent maidens.'

'Heroes don't exist in real life and you've definitely drunk that too fast.' Stefan made a mental note to brief the staff to make her next drink non-alcoholic, otherwise she'd be lying face-down in a coma before the party had even begun.

'You're too modest.' Her eyes drifted from his shoulders to his mouth. 'People are so wrong about you.'

'You are *far* too trusting. What if they're right?'

Apparently undaunted by that suggestion, she closed

her other hand round his lapel and pulled him towards her. 'Do you know what I think? I think you've created this bad-boy image to keep people—women especially—at a distance. I think you're afraid of intimacy.'

Stefan felt darkness press in on him.

She'd found the one tiny chink in his armour and thrust her sword into it.

How? How had she done that? Was it a lucky guess?

It had to be a lucky guess. She didn't know anything about his past. No one did.

'I'm not afraid of intimacy and later I'm going to prove that to you, so don't drink any more or you'll fall asleep before we reach the interesting part of the evening.' Ignoring her puzzled expression, he guided her towards the door.

'I've upset you. Did I say something wrong?'

'What makes you think you've upset me?'

'Because your voice changed.'

Stefan, who prided himself on being inscrutable, started to sweat. Did she pick up on *everything*? 'You haven't upset me but I have guests, and I've already kept them waiting long enough. Are you ready?'

'Yes. Although I'm bracing myself to be hated.'

'Why would you be hated?'

'Because I'm with the hottest guy on the planet. All the women are going to hate me, but don't worry about it. When you're Stavros Antaxos's daughter you get used to not having friends.'

Her tone was light but he instantly thought of the night on the boat, when she'd found a hidden corner to sit, away from all the other guests. She'd worn her loneliness with a brave smile but she'd been almost pathetically grateful when he'd sat down and talked to her.

'Friendship is idealised and overrated. If someone wants

to be friends with you, it's usually because they want something.'

'I don't believe that.'

'You mean you don't want to believe it. You are hopelessly idealistic.' He held the door open for her and the brightness of her expression dimmed slightly.

'So you're saying that true friendship is impossible?'

'I'm saying that the temptation of money is too strong for most people. It changes things.' The scar inside him ached, reminding him of the truth of that. 'Just something to bear in mind for the future if you don't want to be hurt.'

'Is that what you do? Do you live your life protecting yourself from being hurt?'

Stefan, who was used to keeping his conversations satisfyingly superficial, wondered why every exchange with her dived far beneath the surface. 'I live my life the way I want to live it. Right now I'd like to attend my own party. Shall we go?'


Everyone was staring, some discreetly over the top of their champagne glasses and some more openly. But all the glances revealed the same emotion.

Shock.

Feeling like a caged bird suddenly released to freedom, Selene took another glass of champagne just because she could.

Stefan frowned. 'Are you sure you should drink that?'

'Do you know one of the best things about tonight? The fact that all of it is my decision. I decided to come to the party, I decided what dress I'd wear and now I'm deciding to drink champagne.'

'Just as long as you realise you're also choosing to have a crushing headache in the morning.'

'It will be worth it.' She drank half the glass and smiled

up at him. 'Champagne makes everything feel more exciting, doesn't it?'

'The second glass does that. After the third I doubt you'll remember enough about what happened to be excited. I advise you to switch to orange juice.'

'If it's going to give me a headache then I'll find that out for myself.'

'I'll remind you of that when you're moaning in the bathroom.'

She laughed up at him, forgetting the people around them. 'How many glasses of champagne do you have to drink before you'll kiss me in public?'

His eyes gleamed. 'I don't need to be intoxicated for that, *koukla mou.*'

'In that case—' her voice husky, Selene closed her fingers around the lapel of his jacket and closed her eyes '—kiss me.' *Just in case it never happened again. Just in case tonight was the only chance she was going to get to kiss a man like him.*

Anticipation washed over her skin and she waited to feel the brush of his mouth over hers, barely aware of the hum of conversation or the music around her as her imagination took over her mind. But he didn't kiss her. It was a moment of elongated suspense designed to torture her, and just when she'd started to think she was going to remember this moment as the most humiliating of her life she felt the tips of his fingers slide over her jaw.

She opened her eyes and met his, her heart pounding a crazy rhythm.

There was a brief silence and then he slid his hand behind her head and drew her face to his. 'What is it about you? I should walk away, but I can't.'

Desire was an ache low in her belly. 'I'm hanging onto your jacket. That could be the reason.'

He didn't smile. He didn't say a word.

For a breathless moment Selene saw something flicker in those dark eyes and then he lowered his head slowly, his eyes locked on hers. Until that moment she'd never known that a look could have a physical effect, but she felt that look all the way through her body in a rush of heat that spread right through her.

The anticipation was so acute it was almost painful—and he knew it because that sensual mouth curved slightly as he prolonged expectation.

And then the warmth of his breath brushed against her lips and she felt his free hand slide down her back and settle low on her waist as he drew her into contact with him.

She felt hardness and heat and suddenly doing this didn't feel like light-hearted fun any more. In his eyes she saw no trace of humour. Just raw, untamed male sexuality. She realised in a flash that he was controlling every second of this encounter. The pace. The intensity. Even her response. He was in charge of all of it.

And suddenly she knew that exploring her own sexuality with this man was like deciding to buy a pet and choosing a tiger. He was everything that wasn't tame or safe. Everything dangerous. Everything she'd dreamed of during those long nights when she'd imagined her life looking different.

Her mind in fast rewind, she tried to pull away. But his hand was hard and warm on her back and he held her exactly as she'd dreamed of being held.

'Close your eyes, champagne girl.' His soft command slid into her bones and she felt as if she'd just jumped off a high diving board with no opportunity to change her mind before she hit deep water.

And then his mouth touched hers and she forgot all of it as she melted under the skill of his kiss. He kissed her with erotic expertise, teasing her lips with his tongue, driving her wild with each movement of his mouth until her head was spinning and her thoughts were an incoherent blur.

It was, without doubt, the most perfect, exciting moment of her life and she wrapped her arms around his neck, her body quivering as she felt the evidence of his arousal pressing against her.

The fact that he wanted her was as intoxicating as the feelings he whipped up inside her with nothing but the skill of his mouth.

'Maybe you should get a room. I know the man who owns this villa. I could put in a good word for you if you like?'

A light female voice cut through her dreams and Selene would have jumped away from him had it not been for the fact that Stefan kept her locked firmly against him.

'Your timing is less than perfect, Carys.'

'I thought it was absolutely perfect.'

Bitterly disappointed by the interruption, Selene stole a glance at the other woman, wondering who she was.

The woman was stunning, her smile cool as she extended a hand to Selene. 'I'm Carys. And you're Selene.'

It gave her a jolt that someone recognised her. Stupidly, she hadn't even thought of that. 'You know me?'

'Of course. It's just unusual not to see you with your parents. You're such a close-knit family.'

Selene kept her smile in place. This was the part she was used to playing and she played it well. 'It's nice to meet you.'

'Mmm. And you.' Carys raised her glass to her lips, admiration in her eyes as she looked at Stefan. 'I have to hand it to you, occasionally you display a Machiavellian genius beyond anything I've ever encountered. Game, set and match, Stefan.'

Selene, who assumed that this coded exchange related to their relationship, stayed silent as Carys scooped two glasses of champagne from a passing waitress and handed one to her.

'Let's drink to your existence.'

She saw Stefan frown slightly and remembered what he'd said about not drinking any more champagne, but she couldn't bring herself to ask for orange juice in front of this sophisticated woman so she tapped her glass against hers and drank.

The alcohol fizzed into her veins and boosted her confidence. She wanted to dance but no one else seemed to be and when she asked why, Carys looked amused.

'Dancing makes one—hot.'

'Does that matter?' She started to sway on the spot and the other woman smiled.

'That's for you to decide, but if you can tempt Stefan onto the dance floor then you'll have succeeded where others have failed.'

Realising that she desperately wanted to succeed where others had failed, Selene watched as she walked away. 'She hates me. Not because of my father, but because of you. She's crazy about you.'

He gave her a sharp look. 'Not so innocent, are you?'

'I'm good at reading people.' She'd had to be. She'd learned to recognise everything that wasn't said, every emotion hidden beneath the surface, so that she could anticipate and deflect. It was how she lived her life and it was going to take more than one evening of freedom to undo that.

Thoughtful, she finished her champagne. He removed the empty glass from her hand and replaced it with orange juice.

'Here's a hint—alcohol makes you feel good for five

minutes, then you crash and you'll be crying on my shoulder.'

'I only cry when I'm happy. Although you should know I'm very happy tonight so you probably ought to stock up on tissues.' Laughing at the look on his face, she tugged her hand from his and spun onto the dance floor. Emerging from a pirouette, she smacked into Stefan who closed his hands around her arms to steady her.

'No more champagne.'

'Killjoy.'

'I'm preserving my sanity and your brain cells.'

'I just want to start living my life.' The thumping rhythm of the music made it impossible not to dance.

Stefan clamped his arm around her to restrict her movements. 'But you don't have to live it all in one night.'

The music slowed and he drew her against him. She sighed and slid her arms around his neck. 'You know when you have a dream and the reality turns out even better?'

He covered her lips with his fingers. 'I don't know what is coming out of your mouth next, but I suggest this would be a good moment to clamp it shut.'

'It's no wonder all the women chase after you because you are *seriously* hot.'

He shook his head in disbelief. 'Whatever happened to the shy, withdrawn nun who walked into my office?'

'I think this might be the real me, and the real me has never been let out before.'

Amusement mingled with exasperation. 'Should I be afraid?'

'You're not afraid of anything. That's why I came to you. I know it's not politically correct to admit it but I think I might be very turned on by strong men.' Dizzy from the atmosphere and the champagne circulating in her system, Selene leaned her forehead against his chest. 'And it doesn't hurt that you smell amazing.'

'Selene—'

'And you kiss like a god. You must have had hours of practice to be able to kiss like that. It's brilliant to have ticked the first thing on my wish list.'

'You have a wish list?'

'I have a list of ten things I want to experience the moment I leave the island and start my new life. Being kissed is one of them and I have to say you aced that one. I'm so glad it was you and not some slobbery amateur. Another is waking up next to a really hot guy.' She sneaked a look at him and he shook his head in disbelief.

'So this is what happens when an overprotected daughter suddenly cuts loose. Until a few hours ago you were a shy girl who had never been near a city. What else is on this list of yours?'

Selene discovered that her head was too fuzzy to remember in detail. 'Being able to make my own decisions about everything. Sex is on my list, too, obviously. Wild, abandoned sex.'

'With anyone in particular?' His mocking tone made her smile.

'Yes, you. I always wanted the first time to be you.' She saw no reason not to be honest. 'I hope I'm not giving you performance anxiety? No pressure or anything.'

His eyes glittered down into hers but he was no longer smiling. Somewhere during the course of their conversation the atmosphere had shifted subtly. 'I think the champagne is talking.'

'No, I'm pretty sure it was me, although the champagne might have prompted it. It's good at removing inhibitions.'

'I'd noticed.' With a driven sigh, he drew her off the dance floor and down a narrow path that led to the beach.

'Where are we going? You're walking too fast.'

'I'm removing you from public before you tip over the edge and do something you're going to regret.' He cursed under his breath as she stumbled and fell against him. '*Cristos*, I should have taken that third glass of champagne out of your hand.' His voice harsh, he swept her into his arms as if she weighed nothing and continued down the steps. 'Here's another tip. Next time stop drinking while you can still walk in a straight line.'

'There might not be a next time. That's why I'm making the most of this time. You have to live for the moment and I'm living for the moment. At least, I'm *trying* to live for the moment but it's hard to do that unless the other person is doing it too.'

'*Theé mou—*' Jaw tense, he lowered her to her feet and Selene collapsed onto the sand in a dizzy heap.

Shaking her head to try and dispel the swimmy feeling, she pulled her shoes off her feet. 'The world is spinning. Next time I won't drink quite as much quite as fast. And if you even mouth the words "I told you so" I will punch you.'

He swore softly under his breath. 'Do you even realise what could happen to you in this state? You virtually offered yourself to me.'

'I did offer myself to you, but obviously that was too forward of me because now you're frowning. Is it because you don't think a woman has as much right to enjoy sex as a man?'

He sucked air through his teeth. 'I don't think that.'

'Then why are you looking so disapproving? I was relying on you being as bad as everyone says you are.' She flopped back onto the soft sand and he gave a growl low in his throat.

'One of my few life rules is never to have sex with a drunk woman. You should be grateful for that. Stand up!

I can't have a conversation with you when you're lying at my feet like a starfish.'

'Why do men always compare me to animals? First my father says I'm a giraffe and now you say I'm a starfish. The day a man tells me I'm a whale, I'm killing myself.'

With an exasperated sigh he bent and lifted her and she tumbled against him, her body pressed hard against his. There was a tense, throbbing silence broken only by the soft sound of the sea on the sand and his harsh breathing in her ear.

'This,' he breathed, 'is *not* turning out the way I planned it.'

'Tell me about it. I thought amazing things would happen to a girl wearing a dress like this but all I got was lots of anticipation, an incredible kiss and a lecture.'

His grip on her tightened. 'You should be grateful I'm showing restraint.'

'Well, I'm not. I hate the fact you're so controlled. I'd do anything for you to just lose it for a moment and follow your deepest male instincts.'

He muttered something under his breath and then cupped her face in his hands and slanted his mouth over hers. Excitement flashed through her, slid through her limbs and deep into her bones until she felt the strength leaving her. As his tongue traced the seam of her lips and dipped inside Selene felt her tummy tighten and the world spin. His mouth moved slowly, expertly, over hers and she lost track of time and place, *of herself.*

Just when she'd decided that all her dreams about kissing were still intact, he released her.

The sense of loss was searing.

She stared up at him in the semi-darkness, acutely aware of the contrast between them. He was all raw power and masculinity. Despite her height, in her bare feet she barely reached his shoulder.

Without thinking she stretched out her hand and touched his face and instantly heard his sharp intake of breath.

'I'm taking you back to the room.'

'Yes. Take me back to your room so that we can try out your big, beautiful bed. Strip me naked and do unspeakable things to me,' she murmured, running her fingers over his biceps. 'You're very strong.'

'Strong enough to stop you doing something you'll regret tomorrow.'

'You see? You pretend to be bad, but then you're good. I hate to say I told you so, but I was right all along. Secretly you're a nice person, although right now...' Selene suppressed a yawn. 'Right now, I wish you weren't.'

'Stop talking, Selene. Whenever a thought comes into your head, just trap it there. Don't let it out.'

'That's what I've been doing all my life. If my brain is a computer then my hard drive is definitely full.' She gave a gasp as he scooped her off her feet and strode across the sand.

Mouth tight with disapproval, he carried her up a flight of illuminated steps to a private part of the villa. Brightly coloured bougainvillaea tumbled over whitewashed walls and he strode past the small pool she'd noticed earlier outside the doors of the master suite.

'This place is so romantic. Just in case you don't have the energy to make it to the beach, you can leap in here on the way.' Selene gazed at the smooth, floodlit surface of the water, thinking it was the most tranquil place she'd ever seen. Lush exotic plants clustered around the edge of a beautiful pool and the tantalising sound of water came from two elaborate water features. 'How long have you owned this place?'

'A long time.' His voice was terse. 'Can you walk or do you want me to carry you?'

'I definitely want you to carry me. I really like it.' Selene tightened her arms around his neck. 'I want you to carry me straight to bed, and teach me everything I don't know about seduction. We can call it market research.'

'The state you're in, you won't remember any of it in the morning.'

'If it makes you feel better, I'll make notes. I promise to concentrate and learn quickly. You won't have to tell me anything twice.'

'The first thing you should learn is that you should never, ever drink again. The next time you are given a choice of drink or no drink, choose no drink.' Casting her a look of undiluted exasperation, Stefan deposited her in the centre of the huge bed and turned to the woman who had just entered the room. He spoke in rapid Greek as Selene flopped onto her side.

'You're always giving out orders. Does anyone ever say no to you?'

'They work for me. They're paid to say yes. I ordered you a pot of coffee.'

'I can't drink coffee this late. It will keep me awake. Do you give orders in the bedroom?' She sat up and rested her chin on her knees as she watched him. 'Remove your clothes—lie like this—' Her voice was sultry and she saw that his powerful body was simmering with barely suppressed tension.

'*Stop* talking,' Stefan advised in a thickened tone.

Selene watched him hungrily, admiring the sleek, powerful lines of his body. 'Can I ask you something?'

'No.'

'Have you ever been in love?'

'*Stop* talking, Selene. Snap that pretty mouth of yours

shut and keep it shut.' He wrenched off his jacket and slung it on the nearest chair.

'I'll take that as a no.' Her head spinning, Selene flopped back against the soft pile of pillows that adorned the bed. 'I want to be in love. I really, really want to be in love. As long as he loves me back. I would never, ever be with someone who doesn't care for me. That's one of my rules.'

'Does this conversation have a point?'

'I'm just telling you more about me.'

'I don't need to know more about you. I already know all I need to know.'

'So you're a man who doesn't believe in love? I bet as far as you're concerned it's a myth right up there with the Minotaur and the legend of Atlantis.'

'You should definitely stop talking.' Stefan removed his bow tie with an impatient flick of his long fingers. 'Go into the bathroom and turn the shower to cold. It might help you. It would definitely help me.'

She rolled onto her stomach and leaned her chin in her palm. 'Do you know what this room needs? Scented candles. Studies have shown that nine out of ten men are more likely to get laid if there is a scented candle in the room.'

His mouth tightened. 'You know nothing about getting laid.'

'I'm doing my best but you're not being very accommodating.' Trying to distract herself from the spinning, Selene beckoned to him. 'Kiss me. And this time don't stop.'

He stilled, his eyes a dark, dangerous black. 'You are playing with fire.'

'I'd so much rather be playing with you...' Registering the exasperation on his face, she giggled. 'For a sophisticated man of the world with a shocking reputation, you're very restrained.'

'A drunk woman telling me she wants love tends to

do that to me.' Unbelievably tense, Stefan dropped his tie onto a vacant chair and undid the top button of his shirt, his eyes never leaving her face.

'I am definitely not drunk and I absolutely don't want love from you. I just want sex,' Selene said firmly. 'Really steamy sex. There's nothing to be afraid of. I won't hurt you. And you can walk away afterwards and neither of us will mention it again. It will be our little secret.'

The atmosphere shifted in an instant. For a moment she thought he was going to walk out of the room but instead he stared at her for a long time, as if he were making a decision about something.

Just when she'd given up on him taking it any further, he walked towards her with a purposeful stride.

As he approached her tummy tumbled and she felt a wild flicker of delicious, terrifying anticipation.

Her eyes collided with his and she struggled to sit up. 'Say something—'

'You've said more than enough already. It's time to stop talking.' His tone raw, he undid the buttons on his shirt with sure, strong fingers and her mouth dried.

Her stunned gaze rested on his wide shoulders and slid slowly down to his flat abdomen.

'I—I—'

'You issued an invitation, Selene. I'm here to take it up.'

As her eyes fixed on his he shrugged the shirt off his shoulders revealing a bare, bronzed torso that would have been the pride of any gladiator.

'That's what you want, isn't it?'

Still looking at her, he reached for the button at the top of his trousers…

# CHAPTER FIVE

STEFAN lay with his hands hooked behind his head, watching as dawn sent beams of light across the bedroom. He could see a tiny bird dipping itself in the pool, playing innocently, blissfully unaware of the possibility of danger.

It reminded him of Selene.

Next to him, she stirred. With a moan, she flung her arm over her eyes. 'Turn the light off. Ugh—how can you be so thoughtless? It's giving me a headache.'

He turned his head to look at her, remembering how frank and open she'd been. He was starting to understand why her father was so overprotective. She was a sitting duck for any unscrupulous individual that happened to come along.

And now she was lying in his bed.

*His* bed. In his house, where no woman had stayed the night before. The house he'd built from nothing after Stavros Antaxos had ripped everything from his family.

Now he lay in silk sheets, but he never forgot how it had felt to lie on the cold, hard ground with the smell of rotting food in his nostrils. He never forgot the pain of seeing someone he loved laughing with someone he hated.

Stefan reached out and pushed her tangled blonde hair away from her face, remembering how open she'd been with him. It was the champagne, of course. 'It's called the sun. It's morning and your headache has nothing to do with the light.'

She peeled her eyelids open gingerly. For a moment she stared at him, as if trying to work something out. Those eyes slid from his bare shoulders to his abdomen and lower to—

'You're naked?' She shot up in bed and then groaned and immediately flopped back down again. 'Oh, my God, that hurts.'

There was something hopelessly endearing about her lack of sophistication. 'Yes, I'm naked. And so are you. That generally happens when two people spend the night together.' He waited for his words to sink in. Watched as her eyes widened and a faint colour touched her pale cheeks.

There would be regret, he knew. She would shoot out of his bed, accuse him of taking advantage of her and that would be the end of that. Except he would have taught her a lesson life hadn't yet taught her. To be cautious of people.

Next time she'd be more careful.

Next time she wouldn't drink so much with a man she didn't know—especially a man with his reputation.

*Next time she'd know better than to trust someone like him.*

'You undressed me and I don't even remember it.' Her voice was muffled by the pillow. 'I bet that was fun for you. I don't feel too good. Could I have a drink, please?'

'More champagne? That was your favourite drink last night.'

The sound from her throat was a whimper. 'No, *not* champagne. I'm never drinking again. It hurts so much. Why didn't anyone tell me it hurts afterwards? Water. Is there any water? A glass from the pool will do. I don't care. Anything as long as it isn't champagne.'

Stefan reached out a hand for the phone and spoke to someone in the kitchen, all the time aware of Selene burrowed into the pillow next to him like a very vulnerable, very sleepy kitten. She was adorable.

He frowned slightly, realising it wasn't an adjective he'd had cause to use before.

The sheet had slipped. He stared at the smooth skin of her shoulder, knowing that no other man had enjoyed the view he was enjoying now. Unable to help himself, he reached out and ran his hand down the length of her arm, feeling her tremble. But still she stayed in his bed. Even though the alcohol had to have worked its way out of her system, she wasn't showing any more caution than she had the night before.

Tenser than he could ever remember being, Stefan sprang from the bed and grabbed boxer shorts and jeans. 'My advice would be to go and take a long, cold shower.'

'That sounds like a truly horrible idea.' Selene winced as he pulled up his zip. 'Could you try and be a bit quieter? The noise is killing my head.'

And still she lay there. In his bed. In his home. Trusting him.

His fury with her father growing with every passing minute, Stefan dragged open the door of his bedroom suite, removed the tray from his staff with a nod of thanks and kicked the door shut.

Unaccustomed to playing the role of nurse, he poured iced water into a glass and handed it to her.

*Run*, part of him screamed. *Get out of here while you can.*

Still half under the covers, Selene eyed it doubtfully. 'I'm not sure if I'm thirsty after all. My stomach isn't happy.'

'You're dehydrated. You need fluid. And then you need food.'

'How can you mention food at a time like this?'

After a moment's hesitation, he sat down on the bed next to her and scooped her up, keeping his arm around her bare shoulders. Trying to ignore the softness of her flesh beneath his fingers, he lifted the glass to her lips. 'Drink. You'll feel better.' At least one of them would. He should never have brought her back here. It had been an appalling error of judgement on his part.

'I feel hideous. And I hate you for being so full of energy first thing in the morning.' Instead of taking the glass from him, she curled her fingers over his and took a few sips. 'Thank you. You're so kind.'

Kind.

The word jarred against his thoughts.

He felt a rush of exasperation. Somehow he had to kill this impression she had of him as some sort of god. 'You're naked in my bed and you remember nothing of last night.'

'I know. I'm *furious*.'

Stefan relaxed slightly. This was better. 'Good. You *should* be furious with me for taking advantage of you.'

'Oh, I'm not furious with *you*. I'm furious with myself. You kept telling me not to drink. I drank. My fault. How could I be furious with you? You've been amazing.'

'I was the one who stripped you naked.'

'It would have been horribly uncomfortable sleeping in that dress, so I'm grateful to you.'

He'd spent his life shattering women's illusions without trying and now, when he wanted to, he didn't seem able to manage it. Stefan shifted tack. 'It was a *very* exciting night. I am now familiar with every delicious inch of your body, and you,' he murmured, 'are familiar with every inch of mine.'

Still with her hands locked around his, Selene took a tiny sip of water. 'Really?'

'Really. You were so responsive. Unbelievably bold for someone with so little experience. When you suggested I tie you up, I admit I was surprised. I didn't think someone as innocent as you would be prepared to give a man that much power.' He'd expected shock. He hadn't expected a smile.

'I trust you. Whatever you want to do will always be fine with me.' Her simple declaration raised his tension levels several notches. Heat exploded through his body.

'*Theé mou*, I thought you were so trusting because you were drunk, but apparently not. What does it take to get you to show caution?'

'I can be cautious when I have to be. I just don't feel the need when I'm with you.'

'You should be angry.'

'I am angry. Angry with myself for ruining a really special night. You warned me to stop drinking and I didn't listen. You could have left me in a heap on the beach for anyone to take advantage of.'

Stefan couldn't believe what he was hearing. '*I* took advantage of you.'

'No, you didn't. And I'm the one who should be apologising to you for flirting and then collapsing unconscious. Hardly responsible behaviour. You were thoughtful and protective and you lay in bed all night wide awake, frustrated and determined not to touch me because that would have gone against your moral code.'

Why was it that her response was never what he expected? 'Selene, I don't have a moral code.'

'If that's true then why didn't we have sex?'

'What makes you so sure that we didn't?'

'I may be inexperienced but I'm not stupid. I'd know

if I'd had sex. And you wouldn't have done that. Not like that. Not with me. You protected me.'

Her voice husky, she turned her head to look at him and that look contained everything he'd avoided all his life. Depth. He'd always run from it because it led to something he absolutely didn't want. Not ever. He'd seen what that did. Seen lives ripped apart because of it.

'Stop turning me into a hero.'

'You could have taken advantage of me, but you didn't. You could have left me on the beach, but you didn't. You put me safely to bed where no harm could come to me.'

'*My* bed.'

'Where you didn't touch me.'

The rawness of the attraction was shocking. It pulled at the edges of his control, dragging him downwards. He no longer knew who he was protecting—himself or her.

'I was doing you a favour.'

'But you never do people favours, so that makes me feel even more special.' There was a brief pause and then she gave him a soft look that almost finished him. 'You're right. I should take that shower. It will wake me up and make me feel more human.' Her fingers uncurled from his and she slid from the bed, stood for a moment as if she were getting her balance and then walked towards the bathroom.

Naked.

Deciding that selflessness was definitely an overrated quality, Stefan was torn between a desire to flatten her back to the bed or throw a sheet over her. 'You should cover up.'

'What would be the point of that? You were the one who undressed me. You've already seen everything there is to see.'

* * *

She stood under the shower, feeling the cool water wash over her.

The drink and the tablets had cleared her head and reduced the pain to a dull ache. What couldn't be so easily erased was the knowledge she'd messed up what should have been the best night of her life so far. She almost wished he'd lived up to his reputation because then she wouldn't have been standing here bathed in regret.

Switching off the shower, she groped for the towel she'd put out for herself and instead encountered hard male muscle.

Swiping water from her eyes, she opened them. What she saw made her breath catch.

There was nothing tame there. Nothing gentle. Just raw male sexuality.

And he was naked, too.

'Maybe you should have locked the door, Selene.'

His silky voice made her stomach flip. 'Maybe I didn't see the need.'

'No?' He slid his hand behind her neck, his eyes locked on hers as he drew her head towards him. 'You need to develop a keener sense of self-preservation.'

'I can protect myself when I have to.' And she'd had to on so many occasions she didn't want to think about it. That had been her old life, and this was her new one. And because she didn't intend to screw her new life up a second time, she placed her hands on his chest.

His skin was warm. His muscles hard and smooth. The difference between her body and his fascinated her, and she explored him with her fingers and then pressed her mouth to his chest and heard his sharply indrawn breath.

'Are you afraid?' His voice was rough and she lifted her head.

'Excited, maybe a little nervous, but never afraid. Not of you.'

'And if I say that you should be?'

'I wouldn't listen. I make up my own mind. I trust myself.'

He smoothed her wet hair away from her face. 'Your hair is spectacular. You remind me of a mermaid.'

'You've met a lot of mermaids?'

'You're the first.' He lowered his head slowly, his mouth hovering just above hers. 'And I'll be *your* first so if you don't want this you'd better speak now.'

Her heart was pounding. 'I've never been more sure of anything in my life.'

'I do not come with a happy ending attached.' He spoke the words against her mouth, his fingers locked in her hair. 'There's a strong chance I'll make you cry.'

'I only cry when I'm happy. Don't worry, you're off the hook. I take full responsibility. This is my decision.' She felt the warmth of his hand at the base of her bare back as he drew her against him. Felt the hardness of his body against hers and closed her eyes, because she'd imagined it for so long in so many different ways but even her dreams had never felt as perfect as this.

'I might hurt you.'

'You could never hurt me.'

The hand on her back was now resting on the curve of her hip. 'I'm terrible at relationships.'

'I know. I don't want a relationship.' But she wanted *him* and the fact that he was still protecting her made her want him even more. 'I have a whole new exciting life ahead of me and nothing is going to get in the way.'

'You're crazy to do this—you know that, don't you? You should be slapping my face.'

'Stefan, *please*.' She gripped his biceps. 'I want this.

I want *you.* I always have.' He'd been her dream for so long, her lifeline, the one thing that had kept her going when she'd lain awake at night thinking how much she hated her life.

Something in her voice must have convinced him because he scooped her off her feet and carried her back to the bedroom.

The early morning sun beamed approval as he lowered her onto the bed.

Selene didn't care that it was daylight. Daylight meant that she could see him. All of him. Trembling with anticipation, she slid her arms around his neck, drawing him down to her. His hand locked in her hair.

'We're taking this slowly.'

'I don't want slowly.'

'I'll tie you up if I have to.'

'Then tie me up. Do it.'

His eyes darkened. 'You shouldn't say things like that.'

'Only to you.'

'You're far, far too trusting.' Something flickered in his eyes, the suggestion of a frown mingling with the blaze of raw desire.

*If he changed his mind she'd die.*

'Stefan—' Her hands slid down his body and she heard the sharp intake of his breath as she closed her hand around that part of him that was new to her. She·felt silk over steel, experimented with the lightest of touches and heard him groan deep in his throat. The sudden switch of power was as intoxicating as the feel of him. The heady, extravagant excitement triggered by the fact that this man, this gorgeous indecently sexy man, wanted her as much as she wanted him was enough to wipe everything from her head except the moment.

Later she'd think of the future but not now, because right now her dream was finally reality.

'You have to slow down,' Stefan said in a thickened tone, closing his hand over hers to stop her. 'You've never done this before.'

'But I'm learning fast.'

'*Too* fast—' He rolled her under him and brought his mouth down on hers. She felt the erotic slide of his tongue and there was a whoosh of heat through her body that settled itself in her pelvis. The feeling was so maddeningly good that she shifted her hips against him.

He cursed softly and flattened her to the bed. 'You're beautiful.'

Without giving her a chance to answer, he continued his intimate exploration of her body, the wickedly sensual stroke of his tongue driving her wild. Pleasure arced through her as he toyed lazily with the tip of each breast and she wriggled and arched, trying to ease the growing ache low in her pelvis.

No one had told her she was beautiful before but he did so now, again and again, in English, in Greek, and with his lips and hands until she was a writhing mass of sensation.

She hadn't known it was possible to feel this good about herself.

'Stop moving,' Stefan groaned. 'You have no idea how hard you're making this for me.'

It was hard for him? For her it was torture, and when she felt him shift his weight and slide his hand over her quivering abdomen she thought she was going to explode.

'Please, now,' she begged.

He gave a ragged laugh and trailed his mouth lower. 'No way. I'm just getting started, *koukla mou.*'

'But I *really* want you to—'

'I know you do,' he growled, sheer overload of desire

lending an edge to his voice, 'but I want it to be good for you. Trust me.'

She wanted to tell him that it couldn't possibly be anything but good, but the smooth slide of his hand to the top of her thighs robbed her of the power of speech. His clever fingers lingered for a moment, tormenting her and magnifying the ache until she was no longer aware of anything except her own physical need. He touched her *there* and she sobbed with pleasure because he knew everything she didn't and wasn't afraid to show her.

She rocked her pelvis against him and instantly he moved his hand.

'Not yet. Stop moving.'

'I can't.'

'You will. Just lie there. Just—don't move.' He locked his hand round her wrists and lifted her arms above her head. 'Hold on and don't let go until I give you permission.'

Her hands touched the cool metal of the pretty iron bedframe and she curved her fingers around it, holding on as he'd ordered, out of her mind with sheer overload of sensation. She wanted it all. The scent of his skin. The feel of his hands, his mouth, his body— 'Please, Stefan—'

'I don't want to hurt you. I *won't* hurt you.'

'Please—'

'*Don't* speak.' His voice thickened with raw need, Stefan parted her thighs.

She was surprised she didn't feel embarrassed because it was full daylight, but she knew nothing she ever did with him would embarrass her—not even *this*.

*This* was his mouth on her, his tongue on her and in her, and she heard someone sobbing and realised that the sound was coming from her throat. He spread her wide, opening her to his gaze and his mouth, and his only concession to her innocence was his patience. With each skilled slide and lick of his clever tongue the warmth grew to heat, and it spread and consumed her until holding onto the bed felt like holding on for her life, because it was the only thing anchoring her. He demanded everything and she gave him what he demanded because she was no longer in control. He was.

It was almost a relief to feel the first fluttering of her body but he immediately stilled.

'No. Not yet.' His voice was rough. 'Relax. Do you hear me? Relax.'

She was almost crazy with the need and she tried to move her hips against his hand, but he withdrew his fingers from her gently.

'Not yet. I want to be inside you when you come. I want to feel it. Be part of it.'

Her eyes had closed but now they flickered open and she was treated to a close-up private view of sheer masculine power. Dressed, he was gorgeous, but undressed he was spectacular. Bronzed skin sheathed smooth curves of hard muscle and the dark hair that hazed the centre of his chest trailed down over his flat stomach and disappeared out of view. But she'd already seen and she knew, and she wanted to know more.

'Then do it,' she begged hoarsely. 'Do it now. Please. You're driving me crazy.'

'So impatient.' A sexy smile hovering on his mouth, Stefan shifted over her and curved her leg behind his back. 'I'm going to torture you with pleasure,' he murmured against her mouth, 'until you're mindless and begging—'

'I'm begging now.' Her gaze collided with his and every bone in her body melted under the fire in his eyes. 'It's you. You make me—crazy.'

His thick dark lashes lowered fractionally and he lowered his mouth to hers again, his kiss teasing and seductive. 'This is just the beginning.' The subtle stroke of his tongue and his skilled exploration of her mouth left her shaking and Selene kissed him back, her uninhibited response drawing a similar degree of reaction from him.

She was dimly aware that Stefan had pulled back slightly—that he was reaching for something from the table by the bed.

A moment later he slid one hand into her hair. Dazed and desperate, Selene's eyes collided with the fierce passion in his.

'If I hurt you, tell me,' Stefan said thickly, his other hand sliding under her writhing hips as he lifted her against him.

She could feel the male power of him but she was so wet, so ready, and she knew he'd done that for her, done everything he could to make her first time good.

His body felt hard, male and thoroughly unfamiliar. She closed her eyes and held her breath, just waiting, *waiting*, conscious of his leashed power and superior strength and wondering how this could possibly work out well despite his skill.

Braced for discomfort, she was surprised by his gentleness and care.

She'd expected him to thrust, but he entered her slowly, carefully, and she held her breath, the feeling of warmth and fullness taking her by surprise. She felt him pause and then his mouth brushed hers as he kissed her gently.

'Relax and open your eyes. I want you looking at me. If I'm hurting you, I want to know.'

She opened them.

Her heart slamming against her chest, Selene stared up at him, her gaze trapped by his. It was clear how much each slow, purposeful stroke was costing him and Selene slid her hands over his shoulders, feeling tension under hard, sleek muscle.

And then he did thrust, as if he could no longer help himself. He thrust deep and she held her breath because it felt like too much.

Buried deep inside her, Stefan sensed the change in her and paused, his breathing uneven and his eyes darkened to a dangerous shade of black. 'You feel incredible,' he said thickly. 'Tell me you're OK—say *something.*'

But she couldn't speak. Couldn't find any words to express what she was feeling. All she could do was move and when she did that the breath hissed through his teeth.

'I'll take that as an indication that I'm not hurting you.' He groaned, dropping his mouth to hers. His kiss was raw, passionate and hotly sexual, the skilled slide of his tongue winding the excitement tighter and tighter until Selene was aware of nothing except the building tension in her body.

Each controlled thrust of his body was designed to draw the maximum response from hers until the ache inside her grew agonising, her need for him a ravenous hunger that swept away sanity. Heat engulfed her as he drove her towards the peak with a smooth, expert rhythm and then her body tightened and she was launched into an entirely different world, a world that consisted of nothing but her and this man—just the two of them, blended in every way that mattered. Overwhelmed by sheer physical excitement, she was trapped in a vicious cycle of pleasure that sent spasm after spasm of pulsing ecstasy through her thoroughly over-sensitised body and drove him to the same point.

It was the most perfect moment of her life.

And when she finally emerged from that suspended state of erotic intensity, Stefan kissed her gently and rolled onto his side, taking her with him, stroking her hair away from her face with a hand that wasn't quite steady.

'That,' he said hoarsely, 'was incredible.'

Dazed, Selene kept her face against his shoulder, but he gave a low laugh and forced her to look at him.

'You're *not* hiding from me.' He stroked her flushed cheek with gentle fingers, his gaze searching. 'Are you OK?'

Lifting her head, Selene tumbled into that dark gaze. 'I feel amazing,' she mumbled. 'It's better than champagne.'

Humour in his eyes, he drew her head to his and kissed her. *'Much* better than champagne...'

Still dazed by her own shocking reaction to him, Selene closed her eyes.

She'd been worried her dream wouldn't live up to expectation, but it had.

He made her feel utterly desirable, irresistible and beautiful, and she'd never felt like that in her life before—had never imagined it was possible to feel like this. 'Thank you,' she murmured, wrapping her arms around his neck. 'Thank you for making it special.'

He muttered something inaudible in Greek and lowered his forehead to hers. 'I am now officially addicted to your body.'

Selene smiled up at him, feeling like a cross between a goddess and a seductress. 'I think I'm possibly addicted to yours, too.'

'Good. In that case I'm going to break one of my unbreakable rules and keep you here for another night.'

That statement was a reality check. A dark cloud passing in front of the sun. A reminder that this part of her life hadn't officially started yet. *Soon.* 'I can't do that. I have to go home.' Disappointment thudded through her and he lifted his head and frowned.

'Why?'

'I have to get back to Antaxos.'

'I thought you wanted to assert your independence?'

'I do. And to do that I have to go back to Antaxos.' She told herself that was her decision. She was going back for her mother, not her father. And nothing, not even the thought of going home, was going to spoil this moment. Her active mind quickly spun a scenario where she was living here with Stefan, spending her days with her body tangled with his.

She stared up at him, wondering if he was imagining the same thing, but his handsome face was inscrutable.

'Returning home isn't asserting your independence. It's regressing.'

'It's just a temporary thing.' She'd kept her plan secret, protected it as carefully as a mother would her child, desperate for it to grow, but all her defences were ripped away after the intimacies they'd shared. 'I have to get back to the island before my father returns and discovers I've gone. If he knows I came to you it will be difficult for me.'

'Returns?' There was a sudden tension in his shoulders. 'You mean he isn't there?'

'No. Once a year he spends a week on Crete. That's how I was able to get away.'

She wondered why they were spoiling the moment by talking about her father.

She wondered why he was suddenly so still. Why his expression was guarded.

'So you were hoping to return and leave again without him knowing?'

'Of course. Why do you think I came to you? Why do you think I dressed as a nun? He never would have let me leave had he been on the island. I've planned this for so long—you have no idea.'

'Why go back at all? Stay here with me.'

The invitation was so tempting. 'I can't do that. There are things I need from the island—' Years of playing a part stopped her revealing that final secret part of herself. It was how they lived. Pretending that this was normal. Keeping up the show for the outside world. 'Important things. But I don't plan to stay for any time at all. I have to be away again before he returns.'

'Because you're afraid he won't want you to leave? Stand up to him.' His tone cooler, Stefan eased himself away from her and sat up. 'Show him you're a grown-up and he might treat you that way.'

Missing the intimacy, Selene sat up, too. 'You don't know my father.'

'I know that being independent means taking responsibility for your actions and owning them. There is no reason to hide this from him. Tell him you're with me. Show him you're not afraid.'

She *was* afraid. She'd be a fool not to be and she wasn't a fool.

Selene thought about what happened when someone stood up to her father and she thought of her mother, alone and vulnerable on Antaxos.

'I can't do that. Not yet.' The magic had gone so she slid from the bed.

She felt different.

*She felt beautiful.*

She was aware of herself in a way that felt new. And she was aware of *him*. Of the way he watched her as she picked a dress from the clothes he'd bought her. Of the way he looked, his eyes hooded and his jaw shadowed by blue-black stubble.

'Come back to bed. I'll fly you back to Antaxos later if that's what you want. We'll pick up whatever it is you need and then you can come back to Athens with me. I'll help you with your business.'

'I have to do this by myself.'

She walked into the bathroom and turned on the shower, letting the jets of water slide over her body. Closing her eyes, she reached for the soap but he was there before her.

'This soap smells like you.'

She smiled and pushed her soaking-wet hair away from her face as he slid his hands down her body. 'It's my soap. It comes in the same three scents as the candles.'

'At least you know a bit more about seduction now.'

As he kissed her neck she closed her eyes, but this time the anxiety twisting inside her prevented her from relaxing.

Reluctantly, she pulled away from him and grabbed a towel.

'I have to go.'

It felt urgent now, to get this done so that she could start her new life. Excitement bubbled under the feeling of apprehension. She walked back into the bedroom and picked up the pretty linen dress she'd chosen from the clothes he'd provided. Her hesitation was driven by years of living with her father. He wasn't here, and yet she could hear his voice telling her to change into something more suitable. Telling her that the dress was too short, too eye-catching, too—everything.

Then she remembered her father wasn't going to see her wearing it.

From now on the only time she heard his voice would be in her head.

There would be no row because this was the last time she was going home and her father wouldn't be there.

Stefan strolled back into the bedroom, a towel knotted around his lean hips.

Determined not to be distracted, Selene let her own towel drop to the floor and reached for the dress.

Behind her she heard the sharp intake of his breath. Assuming his response was because she was naked, she lifted her head and smiled at him. He was looking at her body.

'*Theé mou*, did I do that? I hurt you?' He was across the room in three strides, his hands gentle on her arms as he turned her and took a closer look at her back and then her arms. 'You have bruises. Finger-marks.'

Selene twisted away from him and pulled the dress over her head quickly. 'It's fine. It's nothing.' It wasn't nothing, of course, but it wasn't anything she wanted him to know about. It was her past and she wanted it to stay in her past.

His face was suddenly pale. 'I thought I'd been gentle.'

'You were gentle. You were brilliant. Honestly, Stefan, it's nothing—' She stumbled over the words, feeling guilty that she had to let him think that but unable to give him an alternative explanation. 'And now I really need to go.'

'You should have told me I was hurting you. I would have stopped.'

'You didn't hurt me.' No way could she tell him, or anyone, the truth—and she didn't need to because she was fixing it. 'I just bruise easily, OK? It's nothing to do with you.' Not looking at him, she scooped her damp hair into a ponytail.

Now that the moment had come, she just wanted it over with. She wanted to get it done. 'I'll take the ferry to Poulos and the nuns will take me back by boat.'

'I'll take you back to Antaxos.'

'No! Someone might see you and call my father. I can't risk him knowing I've left the island. I need a head start on him.'

'Selene—' His tone raw, Stefan dragged his hand through his hair and shot her a look she couldn't interpret. 'He probably already knows.'

In the process of sliding her feet into her shoes, she assumed she'd misheard him. 'How can he possibly know?

He's with one of his women. He won't be home for another six days.'

'He knows because he will have seen the photographs.'

'Photographs?' Selene stared at him, her brain infuriatingly slow as she tried to make sense of what he was saying. 'What photographs?'

'The photographs of us together. You and me.'

'Someone took photographs?' Selene felt physically nauseated. The bag slipped from her hand. 'How could they? This is your home. There were no journalists. Please tell me you're joking.'

'I'm not joking.'

'No—' She felt the colour drain from her face, felt her fingers grow cold and her body sway. She saw the sudden narrowing of his eyes as he saw the change in her.

'I don't see why it would bother you. Nothing else has bothered you. Drinking too much champagne, waking up in my bed, having sex—'

'That's different. My father doesn't know about any of that.' Or at least she hadn't thought he did.

'So this new life of yours only works if your father doesn't know about it? The first step to independence is standing up for yourself. Just tell your father what you told me. That you want to start living your life. You're not asking him for money. You're just telling him how it is.' There was a tightness around his mouth and a coldness in his eyes. 'What can he do?'

Selene knew exactly what he could do. And she knew he wouldn't hesitate to do it.

'How do you even know there are photographs?' *Please let him be wrong.* 'Show them to me.'

Unsmiling, Stefan reached for his phone and accessed the internet. A few taps of his fingers later he was showing her photographs that snapped the leash on her panic.

'Oh, no...' Her voice was a whisper. 'It's you and I. Kissing. And it's a close-up. He's going to go wild. Who took that photo? *Who?*'

'Carys, I suppose.' The question didn't appear to interest him much. 'She writes a gossip column for a glossy magazine and for other places if the story is juicy enough.'

Selene processed that information. 'But if you know she writes a gossip column then you must have known there was a risk she'd take a photograph—that she'd tell the world about me. You must have known—you...' Her voice tailed off as her brain finally caught up. 'Wait a minute. She said something about you being a Machiavellian genius and I had no idea what she meant, but you *did* know. You did it on purpose. You invited me to the party with the express purpose of upsetting my father.'

'I invited you to the party because I needed a date and there you were, all vulnerable and sexy mixed in together—it seemed like the perfect solution.'

'And because you knew it would really upset my father?'

His eyes were cool. 'Yes, I knew it would upset your father. But presumably so did you. If he'd approved of what you were doing you wouldn't have had to come to me in the first place.'

'But I didn't want him to find out yet. It was so important that he didn't find out—why do you think I came to you in disguise?' Realising how naïve she'd been to trust him, Selene took a step backwards, stumbling over his shoes discarded on the floor. 'You warned me—everyone warned me about you—even Maria—and I didn't listen.' Because she hadn't wanted to. Because she'd spun a fantasy in her head and she'd lived with that fantasy for five years and she wasn't going to let anyone destroy it because it had been her lifeline. Her hope. Her dream. 'I thought you were being kind and thoughtful but all the time you were just making sure I came with you so that you could score a point against a business rival.'

His expression was blank. 'This is not about business. I separate the two.'

But she didn't believe him. No longer believed in anyone but herself. 'What sort of a man are you?'

'A man who isn't afraid to confront your father—which is why you came to me in the first place. I am *exactly* the person you knew I was when you walked into my office on that first day.' He snapped the words. 'It isn't my fault if you turned me into some sort of god in your head.'

'Well, don't worry. I don't think that any more.' She choked on the words. 'I can't believe you've done this. This is worse than anything.' Because now she was alone. She was on her own. There was no one out there who would help her. No one who cared. Certainly not this man.

'I've done you a favour. Your father will realise you're serious about wanting your independence. And before you get all sanctimonious can I remind you again that you came to me?' he said flatly. 'I didn't kidnap you, force you into a dress and thrust a glass of champagne in your hand. You were the one who begged me for money and you were pretty much willing to do anything to get it, I might add. If you cast your mind back to your drunken episode my behaviour was impeccable. You did everything you could to seduce me and I said no.'

Humiliation piled onto anger and misery. 'You're just a saint.'

'I never claimed to be a saint. You were the one who came to me in a nun's outfit with ridiculous expectations.'

She stared at him, mute, seeing the uncomfortable truth in everything he was saying. It had been her decision to come. Her decision to drink champagne. Her decision to kiss him and go to bed with him.

She'd wanted so badly to be able to make her own decisions and all she'd done was make bad ones. Lonely and desperate, she'd built him up in her mind as some sort of perfect being and the truth was a horrible blow.

He'd used her to score points against her father and she was the one who would pay the price. *And her mother.*

Thinking of it made her limbs shake. 'You're right, of course. From now on I'll be making more careful decisions. And the first will be to stay away from men like you. That's what you wanted, wasn't it? You wanted me to be more cynical. Well, now I am. I'm officially cynical.'

His features taut, he stepped towards her. 'Selene—'

'Don't touch me. You only invited me to the party because you knew it would upset him.'

'That isn't true. I invited you to the party because you're sexy as hell and your innocence was—refreshing.'

'Well, I'm not innocent any more.'

'You are overreacting. This will be to your advantage. Once he realises you're serious about being independent and making your business a success he'll let you go.' Those wide shoulders lifted in a dismissive shrug. 'I've done you a favour. There's no point in rebelling if no one knows you're rebelling.'

'I've told you this isn't about rebellion. It was never about rebellion.' Selene could hardly breathe as her mind ran swiftly through the possible consequences.

'If you allow your father to bully you, he will always bully you.'

'You have no idea. No idea what you've done. No idea of the consequences that this will have.' Galvanised into action, she stumbled around the room, gathering her things and stuffing them frantically into her bag. 'I have to leave, right now. Is there a ferry from here?' How long did she have? *How long?* She was panicking too much to make the calculation and truthfully it was impossible to know because she didn't know what time her father would have seen the photographs.

He swore under his breath. 'You need to calm down—'

'When would these photos have come out? What time?' Someone, somewhere would have seen them. She was sure of that. Her father was so paranoid and self-absorbed that he had whole teams of people scouring the media for mentions of himself. The moment the images had appeared on the internet someone would have seen them and would have told him. She had no doubt that he already knew everything. Nothing escaped him—especially something as catastrophic as this.

'I don't understand why you're so concerned. I've already told you I'm giving you the money. You'll be able to have the lifestyle you want. Buy what you like without your father's approval.'

All the money in the world would be useless if she couldn't get her mother away from the island. *'What time?'*

Stefan flicked his gaze back to the screen of his phone. 'This one was posted around midnight.'

'Midnight?' Hours ago. And she'd been lying in his bed, basking in the ability to make her own choices, unaware that she'd made nothing but bad ones. Fear gripped her like a nasty virus. She felt dizzy with it. Sick. 'If my father saw these at midnight then that means—' He might already be on his way back to the island and her mother was alone and unprotected. 'I have to leave now.'

Stefan swore under his breath and reached out his hand but she flinched away from him, flattening herself against the wall.

'Get away from me. Don't pretend you care about me,'

she mumbled. 'I know you don't. I don't *ever* want you to touch me again.'

'Fine. I won't touch you.' He spoke through clenched teeth. 'But at least stand still and look at me. The way to handle this is not to sprint home like a good, obedient girl.'

'You have no idea. You have no idea what you've done.'

'At worst I've annoyed your father and reinforced the message that you want to be independent.'

'You might have taken that opportunity away from me—' Her throat was thick with tears. If her father returned home before her, her mother would be too afraid to leave. She'd lose her nerve as she'd lost it so many times before. 'I want to leave. Now.'

'Fine, if that's what you want. Run home. That's clearly where you belong. You're a child, not a woman.' Stefan's face was a frozen mask as he strode across the room and opened a safe concealed in the wall. 'I promised you money. I always keep my promises.'

'Because you're such a good guy?'

'No.' His mouth twisted. 'Not because of that. Call my office any time you need business help.' He dropped the money into her bag and strode towards the door. 'I'll arrange for your transport home.'

# CHAPTER SIX

'STEFAN, are you even listening to me?'

Stefan turned his gaze from the window of his Athens office to his lawyer, Kostas. 'Pardon?'

'Have you heard a word I've been saying? I've been telling you that Baxter has agreed to all our terms. We've been working on this deal for over a year. We should celebrate.'

Stefan didn't feel like celebrating. He listened to his friend offer profuse congratulations, his mind preoccupied with Selene.

What the hell had possessed him to sleep with someone as inexperienced as her?

Her overreaction to the news of the photographs had made him realise how young she was. She'd said she wanted independence, but then freaked out at the thought of her father finding out.

Clearly surprised by the lack of response, Kostas paused. 'Don't you want to hear the details?'

'No. I pay you an exorbitant amount to handle details for me.'

Was it the sex that had made her panic? Remembering the bruises made him shift in his seat but nothing relieved the guilt. He'd never bruised a woman before. A love-bite maybe, but not bruises like those. They were finger-marks, caused by someone grabbing her too roughly, and the worst thing was he had no recollection of doing it.

Kostas closed the file. 'Do you want to meet him in person?'

'Meet who in person?'

Stefan went through their encounter in minute detail, trying to identify when exactly he'd hurt her. He'd been gentle with her. Careful. At no point had he been rough and yet somehow he'd caused those sick-looking yellow bruises.

Yellow bruises. He frowned. 'How old is a bruise when it turns yellow?'

His lawyer stared at him. 'What?'

'Bruises,' Stefan snapped. 'Is a fresh bruise ever yellow?'

'I'm no doctor, but doesn't it take about a week for a bruise to turn yellow? Longer than a week?'

'*Theé mou.*' How could he have been so dense?

Driven by a sense of urgency that was new to him, Stefan pulled out his phone and called his pilot—only to be told that he'd already delivered Selene safely to Poulos, the closest island to Antaxos. From there she'd planned to catch a boat home.

Home, where presumably her father would now be waiting.

Stefan was in no doubt as to who was responsible for those bruises.

That was why she wanted to escape from the island. Not just because she wanted her independence, but because she was afraid for her life. Afraid of her father.

The memories came from nowhere, thudding into his gut like a vicious blow.

*Why doesn't she come home, Papa?*

*Because she can't. He won't let her. He doesn't like to lose.*

The emotion inside him was primal and dangerous.

How could he have been so blind? He was probably one of the few people who knew just what Stavros Antaxos was capable of and yet he'd let his own emotions about the past blind him to the truth of the present.

'He's not going to let her go. He's never going to let her go.' He growled the words and his lawyer looked at him, startled.

'Who—?'

'I'm going to get her out of there.' Driven by emotions he hadn't allowed himself to feel for over two decades, Stefan was on his feet and at the door before his lawyer had even finished his question. 'I'm going to Antaxos.'

'There is no safe landing spot on the island of Antaxos. It's renowned for its inhospitable coastline.'

'I'll fly to the yacht and take the speedboat.' He delivered instructions to his pilot while Kostas caught up with him, following him as he took the stairs up to the helipad.

'What's going on? Is this to do with Selene Antaxos?' When Stefan looked at him, he shrugged. 'The pictures are all over the internet. Why all the questions about bruises?'

His lawyer tone was several shades cooler than usual and Stefan shot him a look. 'I don't pretend to be perfect, but I don't hurt women.' Except that he had. Not with his hands, but with his actions. And by his actions he'd made it possible for someone else to hurt her physically. A cold feeling spread down his spine.

*You have no idea what you've done.*

Her final words still rang in his brain and alongside was a picture of Selene stuffing her new possessions randomly into her battered bag. He'd caught a glimpse of the nun's habit and samples of her soap and candles. But it wasn't the contents of her bag that stuck in his mind as much as the look on her face.

She was a woman who wore her emotions openly and over the past two days he'd witnessed her entire repertoire. He'd seen hope, mischief, flirtation, shyness, wonder, excitement and laughter. This morning he'd seen something new. Something he hadn't understood until now.

He'd seen terror.

Suddenly his collar felt too tight and he called Takis, his head of security, and instructed him to meet him at the helicopter pad.

Kostas caught his arm. 'I have no idea what you're planning, but I advise caution where Stavros Antaxos is concerned.'

Stefan shrugged him off. 'Your advice is duly noted and ignored.'

'You have brought shame upon me and upon yourself and you did it with a man I hate more than any other.'

Selene stood stubbornly to the spot, clutching her bag like a life raft as her father vented his fury. She knew better than to answer back. Better than to try and reason because his anger was never driven by reason. And she was angry with herself, too. Angry for deviating from her original plan. If she hadn't flown to the villa with Stefan she wouldn't be in this position now.

'Why him?' Her father's eyes blazed with every emotion but love. 'Why?'

'Because he's a businessman.' Because he'd talked to her when no one else had. Because he'd paid her attention and flattered her and her stupid brain had built him up into a hero so when he'd invited her to the party it had seemed all her dreams had come true. Instead of questioning what a man like him would see in a girl like her, she'd been blinded by his stunning looks and masculine charisma.

She'd lived in the moment without thinking about tomorrow and now tomorrow had come.

'A businessman? And what is your "business"?' The derision hurt more than any blow.

'I have an idea. A good idea.'

'Then why didn't you come to me?'

'Because—' *Because you'd kill it, the way you kill everything that threatens to break up our 'family'.* 'Because I want to do this by myself.'

And she almost had.

It made her sick to think how close she'd come to a new life.

All of this could have been avoided had she simply shaken hands at the point where Stefan had agreed to give her a business loan, but she'd mixed business with pleasure and even she knew you weren't supposed to do that.

'He used you. You know that, don't you? He used you to get to me and you have no one to blame but yourself. I hope you feel cheap.'

Selene closed her eyes, remembering the way she had felt. Not cheap. Special. Beautiful. But it hadn't been real. He'd done it so that he could get juicy fodder for the photographers. All those things he'd said. All those things he'd done. It hadn't been about her—it had been about scoring points against her father. He'd sacrificed her on the altar of personal ambition. 'I made a mistake.'

'We'll say he forced you. Physically he's much bigger than you, and you're so obviously innocent no one will have any trouble believing it.'

'No!' Horrified, her eyes flew open. 'That isn't what happened.'

'It doesn't matter what happened. What matters is what

people *think* happened. I don't want our family image tarnished with this. I have my reputation to protect.'

Image. It was all about image, not reality. 'He has his reputation, too. And he'll deny it because it isn't true.' Just thinking of that story in the papers made her feel faint because simmering beneath the layers of pain that he'd deceived her was guilt that she'd let him think he was responsible for the bruises.

Her father's expression was cold and calculating. 'Who cares what's true? Mud sticks. By the time he's proved it wasn't the case no one will remember your part in it, just his. People will always wonder. You'll be the innocent girl he used.'

'No.' Selene lifted her chin. 'I won't do that to him. I won't lie.'

There was a deadly silence. 'Are you saying no to me?'

Her stomach cramped. 'I can't do that to him.'

She had money in her bag. If she could just calm the situation there might still be a way to get away. She'd persuade her mother to leave. They could slip away at night. She'd—

He stopped in front of her, too close, his hands clenched into fists that he was getting ready to use. 'So if you liked being with him so much, why bother coming back?'

She knew better than to mention her mother. 'I left because I wanted to have some fun. Freedom. Rebellion.' She made free use of Stefan's misconception. 'I've been trapped here so long with no life and I wanted to get away. But I don't actually want to leave my home. Or my family.' She almost choked on the word because she knew that no family should be like hers. A family was supposed to be a unit knitted together by blood and love. All they had was blood, and too much of that had been shed.

'So you admit you behaved badly?' He flexed his fingers. 'You admit you need discipline?'

The thought of the money in the bag gave her renewed strength. 'I'm sorry my actions upset you.'

'What's in that bag?'

Her knees turned to water. 'Clothes.'

He grabbed it. Wrenched it from her fingers so hard that he tore the skin.

Selene put her hand to her mouth and tasted blood. Inside that bag were her hopes for the future and she held her breath as he wrenched open the zip and dragged out the contents without care or respect, forcing her to watch as every one of her dreams was slaughtered in front of her.

First to fall was the red dress. That beautiful red dress she'd stuffed into her bag in a gesture of defiance against Stefan. She wished she'd left it. If ever she'd needed proof that hope was ephemeral she had it now as her father took that dress and wrenched it from neck to hem. She couldn't even pretend that he didn't know what it meant to her because he watched her face the whole time, and with every rip as she flinched a little more his mouth grew more grim. When the dress was nothing more than torn strips at her feet he kicked the pile of belongings and found her candles.

Selene didn't realise she'd made a sound but she must have done because he glanced towards her swiftly, eyes narrowed, assessing the significance of what was in his hand.

'This is it? This is your business idea? Did he laugh at you?'

'No.' Her lips felt numb. 'He thought it was a good idea.'

'Because he thought he could make a fool of me, not because your business venture has any merit. Is that it? Candles? I'm almost embarrassed a daughter of mine couldn't have been more creative.'

He picked up the apparently empty bag and her heart stopped because she knew it wasn't an empty bag and that if he looked there...if he found...

'That's it,' she muttered. 'There's nothing else there.' And of course by saying that she pronounced herself guilty.

He stared at her for a long moment and then took another look at the bag. With those fat, muscular hands that had turned her mother from vivacious to victim he patted it down and unzipped pockets. And she wished she'd worked harder to hide what was hidden there. Because he found it, of course, under the false bottom she'd created—the thick wedge of money tied with a thong because she hadn't been able to think how else to keep so much cash together.

Her father untied the sexy thong and dropped it to the floor with revulsion. 'You wore that and he paid you in cash?'

'No. I mean...' She floundered. 'The cash was just an advance to—to—'

'To pay for sex.' He put the bag down slowly, his eyes glassy with rage. 'You disgust me.'

'I'll leave. I'll leave and you'll never have to see me again.'

'Leave?' His smile was ugly. 'Oh, no. You don't get to leave. You're part of this family, Selene, and that isn't going to change. This is where you belong and you're lucky I'm prepared to have you back under my roof when you've been with *him*.'

'I don't—'

The blow was unexpected. Because she wasn't prepared, the force of it banged her head against the wall and pain exploded through her skull.

Selene crumpled to the floor, tasting blood. She was so shocked she couldn't move and she fought waves of sickness as his words pelted her like stones.

'Your mother must have known about this.'

*Your wife*, Selene thought dizzily. *She's your wife.* 'She didn't know. I didn't tell her.' Touching her mouth with the tips of her fingers, she realised she'd bitten her lip. She tried to stumble back to her feet but her legs wouldn't hold her and she stayed on all fours like an animal, wishing she'd made different decisions, trying not to feel because feeling was agony.

'When I've finished with you I'll talk to her and she will tell me the truth.'

The implied threat brought her up onto her knees. 'You stay away from her! You touch her again and I'll—' she swayed '—I'll call the police.'

He laughed. 'We both remember what happened the last time you did that.'

Numb, Selene stared at the floor, knowing it was hopeless.

They hadn't believed her. Or if they'd believed her they'd refused to act. Her father was charming, powerful and able to buy his way out of trouble. At first her sense of justice had been shaken. She'd realised that she had no one until one night, lying in the darkness, she'd realised that she didn't need anyone. Maybe no one else could solve this for her, but she could solve it for herself. Which made it doubly frustrating that she'd blown her chance.

He prowled around her and she knew from the look in his eyes that the moment he'd finished with her he would start on her mother.

Something sharp pressed into her hand and she looked down and saw that she'd fallen onto one of the jagged remnants of all that was left of a glass candle-holder.

She closed her hand over it, careful to avoid cutting herself on the sharp edge. And this time when her father came in swinging she closed her eyes and plunged

the glass into his wrist. He gave a howl of pain and stag-
gered backwards. It wasn't enough to stop him but it was
enough to slow him down and Selene didn't waste a moment of her advantage. She forced herself to her feet and
stumbled from the room, slamming the door behind her
as she ran from the villa. He would chase her, of course,
and that was what she wanted. Because if he chased her
then he wouldn't be going for her mother.

She just had to hope that his temper burned itself out
before he killed them both.

Stefan manoeuvred the sleek speedboat as close to the
rocks as he dared. He'd picked the north side of the island, judging the currents to be less savage. His yacht was
moored further out to sea where the waters were deeper
and he'd launched the tender and indulged himself in a few
minutes of speed and spray as he'd skimmed the surface
of the sparkling ocean towards the towering cliffs of Antaxos. But that spurt of adrenaline had been brief. Nego-
tiating the rocky approach to the island had taken all his
skill and concentration.

He let the engine idle as he assessed the distance between boat and rock, judging the rise and fall of the sea.
Between both lay fathoms of swirling water, ready to
swallow up victims, but Stefan had no intention of being
anyone's victim. Judging it perfectly he sprang, lithe as a
panther, landing safely and gesturing for his team to take
the boat back out.

Takis followed him. His movements were clumsier and
Stefan shot out a hand to steady him as he veered danger-
ously close to the water.

'Didn't sign up for this. You could have picked a nice
girl from the centre of Athens, boss,' Takis muttered, his
face scarlet as he found his balance. 'But, no, you had to go

for the pampered princess guarded by the dragon. Working for you is never boring.'

Pampered princess.

Stefan felt a stab of guilt. Hadn't he made the same mistake?

Like everyone he'd been fooled by the image the tycoon had spun for the world. The adored wife. The much loved, overprotected daughter. The happy family.

He suspected the truth was much bleaker. Almost as bleak as this island.

Antaxos.

He stared at the narrow path that led up the cliffs to the grey, fortress-like building at the top.

As a child, he'd spent hours thinking about this place. Powerless, he'd conjured up images of the almost mythical island and imagined himself storming its rocky shores. Something had burned inside him and it burned still, confusing the past with the present.

He wasn't powerless now. He'd made sure of it. From the day his father had brought him the sickening news, through choking tears he'd promised himself—*promised her*—that one day he was going to be a man of power. His quest for that had become the driving force in his life, and when he'd lost his father, too, his drive had simply increased.

A sound made him look up.

Four men dressed in black approached down the path. Bulky men, built like gorillas, whose sole purpose in life was to stop people getting close to their reclusive billionaire boss. If the rocks hadn't killed you, these men probably would.

'This is a private island. You are not allowed to land here.'

Stefan stood his ground, legs spread, using that power

he'd sweated blood to gain. 'You might want to rethink the warmth of your welcome.'

They drew closer. 'There is nothing here for tourists. You need to leave right now.'

'I'm not a tourist and I'll leave when I'm ready.' Timing it perfectly, Stefan removed his sunglasses and the man stepped back. Recognition was followed by alarm.

'Mr Ziakas!' Thrown, the gorilla exchanged a dubious glance with his two colleagues. 'Mr Antaxos doesn't receive visitors here.' But the tone had changed. There was caution now. Respect for the reputation of the man facing them. Respect and just a touch of fear because there were so many rumours about the past life of Stefanos Ziakas. 'You should leave.'

'I'll leave when I have the girl. Where is she?'

They exchanged nervous glances. 'You can't—'

Judging that they were too scared of their boss to be of use to him, Stefan strode past them towards the ugly stone building perched on the hill. His insides churned.

Images blurred in his head and he paused, reminding himself that this was about Selene and no one else.

There was a commotion behind him but he didn't turn his head, knowing that Takis could handle all four of them with his eyes closed. Providing he didn't slip on the rocks and fall in the water.

A faint smile on his mouth, Stefan swiftly climbed the steep path. He was just calculating the most likely place for an overprotective father to lock away his daughter when Selene came flying down a set of steps that led to the path. There was blood on her face, on her hands and streaked through that beautiful pale hair. She was running so fast she almost crashed into him and he closed his hands round her arms to catch her, using all his strength to stop her propelling both of them off the cliff and onto the rocks below.

Her eyes were dazed, almost blank, and he could see now that the blood came from a cut on her head.

Swearing under his breath, Stefan turned his head and ordered Takis to bring the first-aid kit from the speedboat. Then he turned back to her, touching that blonde hair with gentle fingers as he assessed the damage.

Her eyes finally focused on him. 'What are you doing here?'

If he'd been expecting a warm welcome he was disappointed because she twisted in his grip, but he was so afraid she was going to go over the edge of the cliff he kept hold of her.

'Keep still. You'll fall.'

'I know this path. I've lived here all my life.'

And he couldn't bear to think of what that life had been like. 'Did he do this?' The anger roared like a beast but he kept his emotions hidden, not trusting his ability to contain what was inside him.

'You shouldn't be here. I don't want you here. This is *all* your fault.'

'*What* is all my fault?' Stefan tried to ignore the scent of her hair and the feel of her body against his. The hot sun beat down on them but everything else was dark. The rocks, the buildings, *the mood...*

'He saw the photographs. That's what you wanted, isn't it? He was waiting here when I arrived, so if you've come here to do more damage you're wasting your time because there is nothing more you can do than hasn't already been done.'

He didn't correct her assumption that he was somehow behind the photographs. Time enough for that later. His priority was to get her away from here.

Ignoring her attempts to free herself, he examined her

head. A blue bruise darkened the skin around her eye. Looking at it made him feel sick. 'He did that?'

'I fell. I was clumsy.'

She mumbled the words and Stefan bit back his instinctive response to that lie.

'We're leaving, Selene. I'm taking you away from here.'

There was a brief silence and then she started to laugh. 'I came to you for help and doing that made things a thousand times worse. I thought you were a hero—' Her voice broke on the word. 'And just when I find out how far from a hero you really are you turn up here to make things worse. I won't be part of your stupid business rivalry.'

She was so innocent, he thought. Like a child, with a talk of heroes.

She'd stood in front of him in her business suit, spouting numbers and pretending to know what she was talking about, and he hadn't looked deeper. He'd ignored all the instincts that had told him something wasn't quite right. Because he preferred all his interactions to be superficial, he hadn't probed. Like everyone, he hadn't questioned the happy-family image. Even he, who should have known better, had believed it.

'I never claimed to be a hero but I'm going to get you away from here. I promise you that.'

'Forget it, Stefan. If there's one thing I've learned over the past few days it's that the only person I can rely on is myself.'

Before Stefan could respond someone came striding out of the villa and down the path towards them. He recognised the bulky figure of her father.

Stavros Antaxos. Rich, reclusive and rotten. His features were set in a scowl that made closer to bulldog than man and his body groaned from an excess of good food and a shortage of physical exertion.

Stefan topped him by a foot but the other man didn't appear to notice him. His attention was fixed on his daughter.

'You're hurt, Selene—you shouldn't have run. You know how clumsy you are.' His concerned tone caught Stefan off-balance and he realised in those few seconds why no one had questioned the happy-family image so carefully created by this man. He was a master.

His expression was warm and caring as he stepped closer and it was only because Stefan was still holding her that Stefan felt her flinch.

Acting instinctively, he stepped in front of her, shielding her with the muscular power of his body while inside him the anger snapped at its leash. *'Kalimera.'* His voice was silky-smooth and deadly and the older man stopped and looked at him, apparently seeing him for the first time.

His expression altered. Something flickered in those eyes. Something deeply unpleasant. *'Ziakas!'* The other man's face grew ugly. 'You dare show up on my island after what you've done? You made a whore of my daughter. And you did it publicly to humiliate me. You took her innocence.'

Emotion almost blinding him, Stefan was about to answer that accusation with a few of his own when Selene pushed in front of him.

'He didn't take my innocence. *You* did that a long time ago when you became everything no father should ever be.'

Shock crossed her father's face. 'If I've been strict it's because I was trying to protect you from unscrupulous men who would use you to get to me.' His eyes bored into Stefan but Selene shook her head.

'No. You wanted to control me, not protect me. I know what you are, even if no one else will believe it. I won't do it any more. I won't pretend to be this perfect family. It's over.'

Stavros's expression changed slightly. 'You're very emotional, and I'm not surprised. You must be feeling very hurt. Used.'

Stefan saw the confusion on Selene's face and presumably so did her father because he carried on. 'I don't know what this man said to you, but I'm sure it has confused you. He used you to get at me so don't make the mistake of thinking that he cares for you.'

'I know that.' Selene lifted her chin. 'And I used him to get away from you, so that probably makes us equally manipulative. It was my choice to have sex with him.'

Her father moved quickly for a man carrying such excess bulk but Stefan was faster, blocking the blow and delivering two of his own, one low and one straight to the jaw that gave a satisfying crack and sent the other man sprawling on the path.

The Antaxos security team moved forward but Stefan turned his head and sent them a single fulminating glance because now he had evidence of why she'd been so desperate to leave home.

'You really want to defend a man who hits women? Is that in your job description?' When they hesitated, he transferred his gaze to the man now crumpled at his feet.

The man who was responsible for so much pain.

His knuckles throbbed. 'Get up.' Stefan barely recognised his own voice. It was thickened with anger and rage and suddenly he knew he wasn't safe around this man. 'This is what you do to women, isn't it? You live in this place so they can't escape and then you treat them like this. And they don't all get away, do they?'

'Stefan—'

Selene's voice penetrated that mist of fury but he ignored her, all his attention focused on her father.

'I'm taking her away from you. You've lost her. And

I'll be contacting lawyers and the police. The real police, by the way—not the ones you've bribed.'

He watched with a complete lack of sympathy as the tycoon dragged his overweight frame upright, staggering slightly as he stood. Without the support of his security team he appeared to shrink in size.

Stefan turned briefly to Selene. 'Go. Get in my boat. Takis will help you.'

He knew that, wounded and publicly humiliated, Stavros Antaxos was perhaps even more dangerous now than he'd been a few moments ago but to Stefan's surprise instead of denouncing his intention to take his daughter the man appeared to crumple, the fight draining from him.

'If she wants to go she can go, of course. I just want the best for her like any father would. But if she goes then she must live with the consequences.'

Stefan frowned. 'The only consequences will be positive ones. Get in my boat, Selene.'

But she didn't move. Her eyes were fixed on her father. 'I can't.'

He glanced at her impatiently, thinking that he must have misheard. 'What?'

'If I leave, he'll hurt her. That's what he means by living with the consequences. He'll hurt her and it will be my fault.'

'Who?'

'My mother. He'll hurt my mother.' It was a desperate whisper. 'It's what he always does when I don't do what he wants.'

'Your *mother*?'

And then it fell into place, all of it, and he wondered why on earth it had taken him so long to work it out. *This* was why she'd wanted the cash. To get her mother away from the island. And she'd wanted to do it while her father was away in Crete. This was the plan. No rebellion. No business plan. Just an escape plan.

An escape plan he'd wrecked.

She had no other source of income. No place to go. All her resources cut off by this brutal tyrant.

Exasperation that she hadn't told him the truth mixed in with another, unfamiliar emotion. *Guilt?* 'Where is your mother now?'

'In her room.'

With a simple movement of his head Stefan indicated that his head of security should deal with it. Reluctantly, he let go of Selene. 'Do you feel well enough to show Takis the way? If so, go and bring her here.'

Face pale, she glanced at her father and then back at him. It was obvious she didn't know whom to trust and the uncertainty in her face almost killed him.

'Just fetch her.' Unnerved by the blood still oozing from her head, Stefan took a dressing pad from one of the security team and quickly bound her head. 'Stay close to Takis and if you feel dizzy, tell him. I'd go with you but I have some business to finish here.'

Switching from intimidating hulk to pussycat, Takis smiled at Selene and took her hand. 'Which way?'

When they were a safe distance away and out of earshot, Stefan turned his attention back to her father. Turned to have a conversation that was long overdue. Finally he had the power he'd wished he'd had as a child and he used it now, feeling a rush of grim satisfaction as Antaxos's security team melted into the background, not wanting to get between the two men. 'You and I have things to discuss.'

# CHAPTER SEVEN

Numb with shock, Selene sat in the stateroom of Stefan's luxury yacht, watching over her mother.

She knew she had to move but she ached from head to foot after her fall onto the hard floor. Every time she tried to boost her spirits panic descended, squashing her flat. She had nothing. No money, no home, no job, no means to support herself. And the craziest thing of all was that none of that depressed her as much as the knowledge that Stefan had set her up. That nothing about that night had been real.

It was humiliating to admit that she'd been so naïve it hadn't even occurred to her to be suspicious when he'd invited her to attend the party. She'd seen him as heroic instead of as he really was—a ruthless businessman who would stop at nothing to get what he wanted.

He was no better than her father.

She was going to have to try and find someone else to give her a business loan but she already knew her father would block every avenue.

In the midst of her lowest moment ever, the door to the stateroom opened.

Stefan stood there, casually dressed in dark jeans and a shirt that did little to disguise the muscular frame that even her father had found intimidating.

Ignoring the tug of lust deep in her belly, Selene started to boil inside. Misery turned to anger.

How *dared* he stand there, so cool, controlled and *sleek*, when her life was falling apart because of him? Yes, some of it was her fault, but if she'd known what he was going to do she would never have made that decision.

Anger simmering, she stalked through the door and closed it behind her, anxious not to wake her mother and determined to maintain her dignity no matter what.

Determined not to be trapped in a room with him, she chose the steps that led to the luxurious deck, relieved to find that Antaxos was no longer even on the horizon. It was gone and she hoped she'd never see it again.

Stefan strode after her. 'You and I have things to discuss.' He spoke through his teeth, as if he were hanging onto control by a thread. 'But first I want to know why you refused to see the doctor.'

'I don't need a doctor.' She was so shaken by what he'd done she could hardly bring herself to speak to him. 'But you should definitely see one because there has to be something *seriously* wrong with you to even contemplate doing what you did to me.'

The flare of shock in those fierce dark eyes revealed that her response wasn't the one he'd been expecting. 'I rescued you.'

'You rescued me from a situation of *your* making. That doesn't score you any points.' Her voice rose. 'Before St George killed the dragon did he first poke it in the eye with a burning stick and drive it mad so that he'd look good when he killed it? I don't think so.'

Stefan eyed her with the same astonishment he would have shown had the dragon in question just landed on his polished deck. '*You* are angry with *me*?'

'Furious. Livid.'

'Then that makes two of us.' He snapped out the words. 'But before we have this conversation I want the doctor to check you over. You had a nasty blow to the head. Do you have a headache? Blurred vision?'

'I'm seeing you perfectly clearly, Stefanos, and believe me you are *not* looking good.'

His jaw clenched. 'I would appreciate a professional opinion on your health.'

'You need a professional to tell you I'm steaming mad? You can't see that for yourself? If that's the case then you're even more insensitive than I thought.'

His only response to that was a slight tightening of his firm, sensual mouth. 'You received a significant blow to your head. I want him to check that you're all right.'

'Why? Because you care so deeply about my welfare? Or maybe because your master plan isn't finished yet? What am I supposed to do next? Dance naked on national TV?' It gave her some satisfaction to see the streaks of colour tracing the lines of his cheekbones. 'You used me. The whole thing was a set-up—the champagne, the dress, the... the sex.' Why on earth had she mentioned the sex? It was the last thing she wanted to think about. She wouldn't *let* herself think about it. She didn't dare. 'It was all planned so that someone could take the most incriminating photos possible.'

'That is *not* true.'

'That's why you rescued me, isn't it? To score another blow against my father.'

He threw her a simmering glance of raw emotion. 'Stop looking for conspiracy theories. None of this would have happened if you'd told someone your father was abusive.'

'I tried. No one would believe me. We are a happy family, remember? My father is a pillar of society. A philanthropist. He is ruthless, but part of his appeal has always been that he is a family man. People believe that.' She saw from the expression on his face that he'd believed it, too. 'Do you know that he even supports a charity for abused women?' The irony of it almost made her choke. 'I called the police once.'

'And?'

'He told them I was going through a difficult teenage phase. They believed him. Or maybe they didn't—' she shrugged '—maybe they were just afraid of what would happen if they arrested him. Either way, it just made it worse for me and for my mother.'

He turned away and closed his hands over the rail of the yacht. His knuckles were white.

'You let me think I caused those bruises.' The rawness of his tone caught her off-balance. 'You let me think I'd hurt you.'

A sharp stab of guilt punctured her anger. Thrown by the sudden shift in the conversation, she stared at his rigid shoulders and suddenly she was right back in his bed, naked and vulnerable. 'I—I didn't know what to say—'

'The truth would have been good. I blamed myself for being rough with you but I couldn't work out how or when. I went over and over it in my mind.'

'I didn't think it would bother you that much.'

'Why? You think all men like to bruise their women?' He turned, his voice a dangerous growl. 'Is that what you think?'

She shook her head. 'No. I just—I wasn't thinking about you. I was thinking about my mother. If I'd told you the truth you either wouldn't have believed me or you would have tried to stop me.'

'Or perhaps I would have helped you. If you'd mentioned just once when you were presenting your business plan that this was all about escaping from your father we wouldn't be here now. If you'd told me the truth instead of letting me think I'd hurt you—'

'You did hurt me.' Selene felt her insides wobble and reminded herself that everything that had happened between them had been fake. 'I thought you were such a hero. You talked to me that night on the boat. You were kind to me when no one else was. When things were terrible at home, I lay there and dreamed about you. I planned how it was going to be when I finally met you again. How I was going to look. What I was going to say. And every time I imagined it you were the hero.'

His breathing was shallow. 'Selene—'

'And when I finally planned our escape you were part of it. I'd worked through every scenario, making sure that even if it didn't work it wouldn't make things worse. I had a market for my candles, a way of earning money. I was prepared for everything. Everything except a man who lied to me. A man who used me as a pawn in his stupid business rivalry.' Dizziness washed over her like a giant wave and she swayed slightly, resisting her body's attempts to persuade her to lie down.

Dark brows brought together in a frown of concern, Stefan reached for her.

She stepped away from him. 'Do not touch me,' she said thickly. 'Do not touch me ever again, do you hear? You might not have bruised me physically but you hurt me more than my father ever did.' Because she'd cared. Oh, God, she'd really cared. But there was no way she was admitting that now. He'd already had too much of her.

Eyes wary, he watched her. 'You're bleeding.'

'Good. I hope it stains your deck.'

'*Theé mou*, you are the most stubborn woman I have ever met. Will you at least let me change the dressing on your head before we continue this conversation?'

'No. And this conversation is over.' She fixed her gaze somewhere past his broad shoulders so that she wasn't distracted by those killer good looks which could lull a woman into thinking he was a good person. 'All I want from you is to stop at the nearest port. Then you can get back to trampling the innocent as you build your empire. You and my father are each as bad as the other.'

'I'm not dropping you anywhere. Your father is being arrested as we speak. He'll be charged but we can't be sure he won't be released. As you rightly say, he has powerful friends. You're staying with me and that's non-negotiable. Now, sit down before you fall down.'

Yesterday she would have taken his words to mean he wanted her with him but she knew better now.

'If you're planning on keeping me for leverage against my father I can assure you he won't care what you do.'

'That is *not* what I was thinking.'

'Of course it wasn't. You'd never use a person like that, would you, Stefan?'

'Selene—'

'Just so that we're clear about who we're dealing with, he isn't going to care if you throw my dead body over the side of your boat even if you've packaged me in red sequins and a bow.' She was horrified to discover a lump in her throat. 'My father doesn't love me and never has.'

What was it about her that was so unlovable?

Knowing that this wasn't the time to dwell on that, she blinked and cleared her vision. But it was too late because he'd seen and instead of backing away, which was what she would have preferred, he moved closer.

His hands were gentle on her face, tilting it as he urged her to look at him. 'If that is the truth then you are better off building your life without him. I will help you do that.' The softness in his voice almost finished her.

'No, thanks. I've already experienced your idea of "help". From now on I help myself. I don't want anything to do with either of you.'

'You're not thinking the situation through. You have nowhere to go.'

The fact that it was true did nothing to improve her mood. Panic squeezed her insides. 'I wouldn't stay on this boat with you if it were the only piece of dry land in the Mediterranean. I'd rather be eaten by sharks.'

'That's extremely unlikely in these waters.'

'Are you mocking me?'

Her voice rose and he went unnaturally still.

'No. I'm merely trying to stop you making a rash, emotional decision that will harm no one but yourself.'

'So now you're saying I'm rash and over-emotional?'

'*Cristos*, stop twisting everything I say! If you had told me the truth I would have ensured your safety. And that is enough of the past. You need to think about the future. I'm willing to offer you and your mother a home—on a temporary basis, of course,' he added swiftly, 'until you can find somewhere suitable.'

Selene heard that hastily added qualifier and burst out laughing. 'I'm almost tempted to say yes. It would serve you right to find yourself living with a woman *and* her mother. That would really cramp your style. Relax, Stefan. I can't think of anything worse than living under the same roof as you.'

His jaw was clenched. 'It's probably wise to stop talking while you're this upset because you're going to say things you don't mean.'

'I mean every word.'

'I'm trying to help you.'

'You're the one who taught me to be cautious.' Her gaze lifted to his shoulders, travelled over the bronzed skin at the base of his throat and finally met those dark eyes that could seduce a woman with a single glance. 'I don't want your help. I never want to see you again.'

Below deck in the owner's suite, Stefan poured himself a large drink, but when he lifted it to his mouth his hand was shaking so badly the liquid sloshed over the side.

Cursing softly, he put the glass down and closed his eyes, but that didn't help because his mind was tortured by images. Images of her stepping back onto the island not knowing whether her father was waiting. Images of his anger spilling over. Images of that beautiful hair streaked with blood.

Gripping the glass, he drank, feeling the fire burn his stomach.

While he'd been on the island he hadn't dared let himself feel, but he was feeling now and the emotion hit him so hard he couldn't breathe. He'd never let it out before and because he'd never let it out he had no idea how to haul it back inside again.

Business rivalry. She thought this was about *business*?

He had no idea how much time had passed but eventually he heard a voice behind him.

'Boss?'

It was Takis.

Not willing to reveal even a sliver of weakness, Stefan kept his back to him. 'Problems?'

There was a brief pause. 'Possibly. The girl and her mother have gone.'

'Gone?' He was surprised how normal he sounded. Surprised by the strength of his voice given the turmoil inside him. 'Gone where?'

'Left the boat, boss.'

'How can they have left the boat? Did they swim?'

'Er—the boat docked twenty minutes ago, boss.'

Docked?

Stefan turned his head, saw the port, and realised with a stab of shock just how long he'd been down here. While he'd been trying to get himself under control they'd arrived in Athens.

'How can they have gone?'

'No one was looking, boss.'

Stefan rolled his shoulders to ease the tension. 'You are telling me that two women, at least one of whom was in a weakened state, managed to leave my boat unobserved by any of my so-called security team within two minutes of arriving at Athens?'

'It would seem so. I take all the blame.' Takis sounded sheepish. 'Fire me. Truth is, I wasn't expecting them to leave. Selene is a very determined young woman. I underestimated her.'

'You're not the only one guilty of that.' Stefan stared blindly out of the window, knowing that the blame was his.

Instead of listening, instead of proving he was someone she could trust, he'd been angry—and she had no way of knowing that the root of that anger had nothing to do with her.

No wonder she'd walked.

She'd had enough of male anger to last her a lifetime.

Takis cleared his throat. 'I'm worried he might go after her, so I've already got a team on it and I've briefed a few people. Called in a few favours. We'll find her.'

Stefan knew that the Ziakas name had influence. He had links with everyone from the government to the Athens police. But he also knew better than to underestimate his enemy, and in this case his enemy was formidable and motivated.

Stavros Antaxos wanted his wife and daughter back

and he had a web of contacts every bit as impressive as Stefan's.

Takis was watching him. 'Have you any idea where she might go? Any clues?'

Where could she go? How did she plan to support herself?

She'd left the island with nothing. Not even the battered old bag holding her candles and soap and the money he'd given her.

Tension rushed into his shoulders. She had no one to defend her. No way of earning money.

He imagined some unscrupulous man handing her a drink. Imagined him being on the receiving end of that sweet smile and quirky sense of humour. Imagined her naked with another man—

Sweat broke out on the back of his neck and he uttered just two words.

'Find her.'

# CHAPTER EIGHT

THREE weeks later Selene was balancing plates in a small *taverna* tucked away in the labyrinth of backstreets near the famous Acropolis when she heard a commotion behind her.

'Hey, Lena, take a look at *him*,' breathed Mariana, the waitress who had persuaded the owner to give Selene a job when she'd appeared out of nowhere only hours after she'd slipped away from the luxurious confines of Stefan's yacht. 'That man is smoking hot. He should come fitted with air-conditioning.'

Terrified of losing concentration and dropping the plates, Selene focused on her task until the meals were safely delivered to the table. 'Two *moussaka*, one *sofrito* and one *kleftiko*.' She was so nervous of doing something wrong and losing her job she didn't even look to see who was attracting everyone's attention and anyway, she'd had enough of 'smoking hot' men. 'Can I fetch you anything else?'

'Just that indecently sexy Greek man who has just taken the table behind you, honey,' the woman murmured, her eyes fixed in the same direction as Mariana's. 'Do they all look like that around here? If so, I'm moving here. No question.'

'That would be great for the economy.' Selene added

fresh cutlery to the table and removed empty glasses. On her first day she'd dropped a tray. It had only happened once. She'd learned to balance, concentrate and not over-load. 'How are you enjoying your holiday? Did you make it to Delphi yesterday?' This was the part of the job she loved most of all—talking and getting to know people, especially when they returned to the *taverna* again and again. She'd used her mother's maiden name and no one knew who she was. The anonymity was blissful, but no-where near as blissful as being able to live her life the way she wanted to live it. 'I'm going there on my next day off.'

'We followed your advice and went early in the morn-ing. It was perfect. It's always good to have local knowl-edge.'

Knowing that her 'local knowledge' had been rapidly acquired over a three-week period, Selene smiled. 'I'm glad you had a good time.'

'We did. And talking of good times—' the woman peeped over the top of her sunglasses '—that guy makes me want to forget I'm married. If he's looking for com-pany, send him my way.'

A nasty suspicion pricking the back of her neck, Selene turned and glanced towards the man who was attracting so much attention.

Stefan lounged at a table in the far corner of the *tav-erna*. Even without the expensive suit there was an un-mistakable air of wealth and power about him, and yet she knew women stared not because of the promise of riches but because his raw masculine appeal promised sex as they'd never had it before. He attracted women like iron filings to a magnet with no apparent effort on his be-half. Perhaps that was why, she thought numbly. Perhaps it was his supreme indifference that provided part of his appeal. Every woman wanted to be the one to catch the attention of a man whose attention wasn't easily caught. There wasn't a woman alive, even those happily married, who could look at this man and not wonder what a night with him would be like.

And *she* knew.

His gaze locked on hers and she knew her changed appearance hadn't fooled him for a moment. In that single look she was hit with the full force of his masculinity. Her body burned under his steady appraisal but even though she wanted to she couldn't look away.

Something passed between them. Something raw and primal that made it impossible to think of anything but those intense, unforgettable hours she'd spent in his bed.

Desperately, she tried to remind herself that none of it had been real. At least, not for him.

'Kalimera.'

He spoke softly and Selene almost stumbled, tightening her grip on the tray to stop it from crashing to the ground.

It wasn't fair that she should feel like this.

By rights she should be able to look at him and want to slap his face. Instead all she wanted to do was grab the front of his exquisitely tailored shirt with both hands and rip it open, exposing the man underneath. On the surface he seemed so urbane and sophisticated—*civilised*—and yet beneath the trappings of success was a man who had fought his way to the top with his bare hands. He had no scruples about doing what needed to be done to get what he wanted. Of course he didn't. He ran his business according to his own agenda with no thought for anyone else. He'd used her to score points against her father. Knowing that, she wanted to look away, but those dark, dangerous eyes wouldn't release her from that invisible bond that held her trapped.

Her brain appeared to have shut down and she was

breathing so fast she started to feel light-headed. 'What are you doing here?'

'Pausing for a drink in a local *taverna* after a long, stressful day at work.' He stretched out his legs, as relaxed as she was tense, those dark eyes watchful.

'Why pick this one?'

'You already know the answer to that.'

Why would he have tracked her down? Why go to that trouble?

She could feel everyone watching them, straining to hear the conversation. Saw her boss watching her with a frown and remembered just how precious this job was. 'What can I get you?'

'Just coffee.' Somehow he managed to make that instruction sound intimate. 'I like your hair. The cut shows off your face.'

The compliment threw her and she lifted her hand to her newly cropped hair.

She'd cut it herself, with blunt scissors and nothing but a chipped mirror in which to view the results. With a few hacks of those scissors she'd become Lena. And when she'd finished hacking she'd scooped up the mounds of soft golden hair and added them to the rubbish where no one would find it. It was the first thing she'd done in her new life. The second was to get a job, and she knew she'd been lucky to get this one when so many were struggling.

'What do you want, Stefan?'

'You didn't have to cut it. You don't have to hide.'

Panic gripped her and she glanced over her shoulder to check no one was listening. 'I'm not hiding. I'm working in a restaurant in full daylight. And I'd like to take your order.'

'You're trying not to draw attention to yourself. You've cut your hair. You're nervous. I can protect you.'

There was a strange fluttering low in her belly. 'Too late. I don't believe in heroes any more.'

'How about man's ability to make a mistake. Do you believe in that?'

She didn't dare listen. He was smooth, persuasive and a master negotiator. She knew he would probably be capable of convincing her of anything.

'I'll fetch your coffee.'

'What time do you finish?'

'It doesn't matter. I don't want you to come here again. You *mustn't* come here again. You're too—conspicuous.' Her heart thudded hard against her ribs. The thought that her father might find her made her feel sick. She'd contemplated hiding away but that would have made it impossible for her to work, and if she couldn't earn money she couldn't be independent. And that wasn't all, of course. She refused to live her life in hiding.

He read her mind and his gaze darkened. 'I won't let him hurt you.'

'You were the reason he hurt me last time. If you come here, you'll attract attention. I don't want you here again.'

He reached out, those long, strong fingers trapping hers. 'I repeat—he won't hurt you.'

'And how do you plan to stop him? I'd rather rely on myself, thank you.'

'The police questioned him and then released him. You haven't been out of our sight for the past three weeks.'

The shock was physical. She snatched her hand away from his. '*Our* sight?'

'I had to ensure your safety. As you pointed out when we last met, my actions put you in danger. The least I could do was fix that. He won't touch you again.'

'You've had me followed?'

'For your safety.'

The thought made her grow cold. He'd had her followed and she hadn't noticed. She'd been alert, on the look-out, but she hadn't noticed. How could that have happened?

She looked around but no one stood out. There were tourists. A group of Americans. An English couple. A bunch of local men. Two giggling teenage girls. 'How? Who has been watching me?'

'You wouldn't have seen them so stop beating yourself up for being unobservant.'

'I've been looking.'

'Takis only employs the best in his team. If you'd spotted them they would have been out of a job.'

*Takis.* Selene remembered how kind he'd been to her mother that day. How kind he'd been to her. 'He's…' She sighed. 'I liked him.'

'I only employ the best, too. As I said—you don't need to be afraid.'

'I'm not afraid. And I don't appreciate you interfering.'

'You accused me of putting you in danger. You have to allow me to put that right.' His tone was conversational. Casual. No one watching them would have guessed they were talking about anything more significant than the menu.

'If you don't want to put me in danger the best thing you can do is stay away.'

'We'll talk about it over dinner, Selene.'

'No way.'

'Last time we spent an evening together we had fun.' He hesitated. 'I want to see you again.'

The air left her lungs in a rush and she was so shocked she simply stared at him. Terrified that someone might have overheard, she didn't dare look at anyone. 'The last time we spent an evening together you ruined my life. And my name is Lena. I'll fetch your coffee.' She backed away from him, knocking into the table behind her.

*The last time we spent an evening together we had fun.*

Those words sent images rushing back into her head. Images she'd been trying to delete for the past three weeks.

She walked briskly back inside the *taverna*, shaking so badly she was convinced everyone would notice.

Fortunately they all seemed too overawed by the identity of their illustrious visitor to pay any attention to her pale face.

'Everything OK?' Mariana walked up to her, her cheeks pink from the heat. 'It's a hot one today, that's for sure.'

A rowdy group of young men took a table near to them and Selene took a step towards them, but Mariana stepped in front of her in a smooth move.

'I'll take them. They look as though they've had a bit too much to drink already. Just my type.'

Selene frowned. 'I can handle it.'

'You serve Ziakas. He's more important. Plenty of people round here wish he'd give up running his company and run Greece. He'd soon sort out our problems. You only have to look at him to know there is nothing that man doesn't do well.'

Selene stared at her for a moment, wondering how she could have been so obtuse. 'You work for him. *You're* the one who has been watching me.'

Mariana hesitated and then shrugged. 'One of them. I don't see why it has to be a secret. If a man was going to all this trouble for me, I'd want to know. I mean, the guy has done everything except call in air support. He obviously adores you.'

'I thought we were friends?'

'We are friends. Just because I'm an expert in hand-to-hand combat doesn't mean I can't have female friendships.'

Selene's head was reeling. 'So you're—?'

'Ex-military. But fortunately I also make a mean cap-
puccino. It's a useful skill.'

Mouth tight, Selene picked up the coffee order from the
counter and thrust the cup to Mariana. 'In that case you
can serve him. He's your boss.'

'A few layers above me. Technically I work for Takis. I
don't understand why you're upset.' Mariana's expression
was curious. 'The guy has virtually enlisted the Marines to
keep you safe. And he is so tough. If a guy like him were
that keen on me I wouldn't be complaining. Unfortunately I
only attract losers and once they discover I can break their
arm with one twist they run away terrified. No idea why.'

'He's not keen.'

'Right. So he's going to all this trouble just for his en-
tertainment? I don't think so.' Marianna added a spoon
to the saucer. 'Why not just go out with him a few times?
Have some fun with his bank account?'

'The problem with rich guys,' Selene said tightly, 'is that
they think all that money gives them the right to trample
all over you.'

Mariana's gaze slid to Stefan. 'He can trample on me
any time he likes. Sadly he hasn't looked once in my direction and that's because he can't stop looking at you.
Are you seriously not going to do anything about that?'

'No, I'm not. Tell me one other thing—did he arrange
for me to have this job?'

Mariana pulled a face. 'I—'

'Great. So I didn't even get this on my own merits.'
Furious, confused, she walked over to the group of men.
'What can I get you?'

They were rowdy but good-natured, and this was their
third trip to the *taverna* in the same week so she recognised them immediately.

'Hey, Lena—' one of them winked at her '—what are the specials tonight?'

She told them, handing out menus and taking their drinks order, shifting slightly to one side when the man's hand covered her bottom.

'I recommend the lamb.'

'We're going clubbing later. Will you come?'

'I'll be too tired after working here all day, but thanks for the invitation.' She was used to deflecting invitations and she kept it light and friendly, kept the smile on her face, all the while aware of Stefan seated two tables away, listening to every word.

She felt him watching her. Felt those sinfully sexy eyes following her every move as she moved between tables serving tourists and locals.

He sat still as Mariana delivered his coffee, and continued to watch Selene until her nerves were shredded and she hardly dared hold a plate in case it slipped from her sweaty fingers.

The fact that they'd been watching her without her knowledge freaked her out.

Who else was watching her?

Suddenly she made a decision.

Walking through to the bar area, which couldn't be seen from the restaurant, she smiled sickly at the owner and told him she was feeling unwell. The job wasn't real anyway. He'd only given her the job because the Ziakas machine had swung into action.

She went to the bathroom, pushed open the window, climbed through it and dropped onto the street outside.

Brushing off the dust, she derived some small satisfaction from the knowledge that she wasn't making it easy for him. No doubt he'd track her down again in no time if he wanted to, but that didn't mean she had to hand herself over.

Heart pounding, she sprinted along the maze of streets that led back to the tiny room she was renting, all the time expecting to hear the heavy tread of masculine footsteps behind her.

She was just congratulating herself on successfully slipping away when a male hand curved over her shoulder.

Terrified that it might be her father or one of his men, Selene turned round swinging but it was Stefan who caught her arm.

'It's all right. It's just me.' His voice was roughened with concern. 'But it might not have been. Why are you doing this to yourself? Why are you making it hard for us to protect you?'

'I've been followed and watched over for the whole of my life. I am trying to escape from that.'

'I offered you my help but instead you choose to spend your day working in a *taverna* being propositioned by sleazy men in Hawaiian shorts.'

'And what are you, Stefan? A sleazy man in an expensive suit? At least they're honest about what they want.' Still shaken by the panic that had gripped her when he'd touched her shoulder, she pressed herself against the wall. 'I really have no idea why you're even here. I've served my purpose and we both know you're not interested in anything or anyone unless it serves a purpose.'

'Since when did you become so cynical?'

'Since I accepted that you're a cold, emotionless megalomaniac with no redeeming qualities. Now, if you'll excuse me, I'll—'

'No.'

He planted his arms either side of her, caging her, and she gasped, shoving him hard.

'Don't *ever* trap me like that.'

'Then don't run.' But he lowered one of his arms. It made virtually no difference because he was standing so close to her there was no way she could move. 'I did *not* invite you to that party because of your father. I invited you because you were sweet and sexy and because I wanted to spend time with you.'

'I don't want to talk about this. It's too late, Stefan.'

'Journalists take photographs of me all the time. It's part of my life. So much a part of it I didn't think of it. Had you explained to me the importance of your father not knowing, it might have occurred to me.'

'I arrived in your office in disguise. Didn't that give you a clue?'

'You told me he disapproved of what you were doing and I had no reason not to question that. You were dressed in a nun's outfit—' his eyes gleamed with self-mockery, '—I assumed that what came out of your mouth was the truth.'

'But you knew I wanted to keep my visit to you a secret.'

'I didn't even think about it. There is a world of difference between a disapproving father and an abusive father. I thought you wanted to make your mark on the world. I didn't know he was leaving marks on you.' There was a brief pause. His mouth tightened. 'You should have shared that with me.'

'Apart from that one abortive attempt to tell the authorities, I've never shared it with anyone.'

'But you shared something else with me you've never shared with anyone.' His fingers brushed her cheek, surprisingly gentle. 'You could have trusted me, Selene.'

She felt her body respond instantly and knew that the biggest danger to herself came from him.

'So you're saying what happened is my fault?'

'No, it was mine.' His hand dropped. 'And I apologise because the possibility of photographs should have occurred to me and it didn't. But the reason it didn't was because I've lived with it for so long I don't notice it any more.' His leg brushed against hers. Her mind blurred.

Melting inside, Selene pressed herself hard against the wall in an attempt not to touch him. 'It really doesn't matter. I've moved on.'

'But you've moved on without me,' he said softly, 'and that isn't what I want. Your mother seems well.'

'She's very well. She's been staying in the same artists' community she lived in when she first arrived in Athens as a teenager. She's painting again and her confidence is returning. It's wonderful to see that after—' She broke off, eyes wide. 'Wait a minute, how do you know she's well? You've followed her, too?'

'Naturally we are concerned. Unlike you, she welcomes the protection. It has allowed her to relax and enjoy her new life and her old friends.'

Selene thought about how frightened her mother had been. 'All right—' her voice sounded stiff '—maybe I'm grateful to you for helping my mother, but don't think it's going to change the way I feel about you.'

'You're very cynical all of a sudden, *koukla mou*. It doesn't suit you. It isn't who you are.'

'It is now. And it was being with you that made me this way.'

'So you've changed personality in a matter of weeks? I don't believe that. You are the most open, trusting person I've met.'

'You mean I'm stupid.'

A frown touched his brows. 'No. I do not mean that.' He took a deep breath. 'I realise we have some obstacles to overcome, but it would be much easier to overcome them if I wasn't worrying about your safety all the time. I want you to come and stay at my villa, at least for a while.'

The temptation was so great it horrified her. 'No, thanks.'

'I don't want you living on your own.'

'Well, I want it. I've lived under my father's rules for so long I want the freedom to come and go as I please. I can wear what I like. See whoever I like. Be who I want to be.'

'And who do you want to be?'

She'd thought about nothing else.

'Myself,' she said simply. 'I want to be myself. Not someone else's version of who they think I should be.'

'So if I ask you—the real you—out to dinner, will you say yes?'

Selene swallowed, unsettled by how much being this close to him affected her. What scared her most in all this was how badly she lost her judgement around him. She didn't want to be the sort of woman who lost her mind around a man. 'Why are you bothering? Why are you so persistent?'

'When there is something I want, I go for it. That's who I am.'

'And you're pretending that's me? Come on, Stefan, we had one night. A whole night. I'm already the longest relationship you ever had.'

'And I'm the only relationship *you've* ever had.' His eyes were dark and not once did they shift from hers. 'Are you telling me you don't want to explore that? Are you telling me you don't think about it?'

The heat went right through her body. 'I try not to because when I remember I also remember how you used me to score points with my father.'

A muscle flickered in his jaw. 'You don't believe that it was not intentional?'

'No, I don't.' She didn't dare. She was *not* going to be gullible. 'I think you're trying to talk your way out of trouble.'

He stared down at her for a long moment. 'Even if you don't want to eat with me you're working yourself to the bone trying to afford to live. Let me help you.'

'I don't need or want your help. I'm doing fine by myself.'

'Working in a *taverna*?' He lifted his hand and touched her cropped hair. 'What about your scented candles? What happened to the dream?'

'The dream is still there. I'm working to get the money I need to set up in business.'

'You're determined to do things the hard way?'

'I'm determined to do things myself.'

'I said I'd give you a business loan. That offer still stands.'

'I no longer want anything from you.'

His gaze was suddenly thoughtful. 'You're worried you can't control your feelings around me?'

'You're right about that. There's a possibility I could punch you. I can't be sure it won't happen.'

For some reason that made him smile. He stepped back and glanced up at the run-down building. 'This is where you're living?'

'Where I'm living is none of your business. Neither is where I'm working or who I'm seeing. This is my life now and I'm not sharing the details with anyone.'

His mouth tightened as he took in the paint blistering on the woodwork. 'I want to help you and that help is not linked to what happens between us.'

'Nothing is going to happen between us. Next time I get involved with someone it will be with a man who has strong family values and who doesn't treat commitment as a contagious disease to be avoided at all costs.'

'Family. You still believe in family after what he did to you?' Lifting his hand, he traced her lower lip with his thumb, a brooding look in his eyes. 'Love just makes you vulnerable, *koukla mou*. You are hurting because you loved.'

'I'm not hurting.'

'I saw your face that day on the island. I saw the way you looked at him.'

'He's my father. You can't just undo that.' How did they come to be talking about this? It was something she'd never talked about, not even to her mother. It felt wrong to want love from someone for whom you had no respect. 'But it's—complicated.'

'Emotions are always complicated. Why do you think I avoid them?'

Despite herself, she found herself wondering about him. She saw the shadow flicker across those moody eyes and the sudden tension in his shoulders as he let his hand drop.

'My advice? Forget your father. He isn't worth a single tear from you. And as for family—' he eased away from her '—travel through life alone and no one can hurt you.'

His words shocked her. 'Thanks to my father I've been alone for the best part of twenty-two years and that sucks, too. He alienated everyone. My life was a lie. For the first time ever I'm making friends and I'm loving it. No one knows that my surname is Antaxos. No one cares. I'm Lena.'

A noisy group of tourists surged down the narrow street and she flinched.

He noticed her reaction instantly. 'And you're looking over your shoulder all the time. Come with me and you won't have to look over your shoulder.' He stepped closer to her, protecting her from the sudden crush of people. His thighs brushed against hers and her stomach clenched. 'I can protect you from your father.'

But who would protect her from Stefan?

Suffocated by the feelings inside her, Selene lifted her head and their eyes met.

The noise of the crowd faded into the background and all she could think was that he was the most insanely good-looking man she'd ever seen. And then he was kissing her, his mouth possessive, skilled, explicit as he coaxed her lips apart in echoes of what they'd shared that night at his villa.

When he finally lifted his head she had to put her hand on his chest to steady herself.

'I want to start again,' he said roughly, cupping her face in his hands and lowering his forehead to hers. 'I've never felt this way about a woman before. Everything that happened between us was real. All of it. And deep down you know it. Give me a chance to prove it to you.'

His body was pressed up against hers, and it was an incredible body. Hard muscle, height, width—he was exquisitely proportioned. Even though the night was oppressively warm, she shivered.

He lifted a hand to her short hair, toying with the ends. 'I'm attending a charity ball tomorrow on Corfu. It's going to be glamorous. Men in dinner jackets, champagne in tall, slim glasses. Your kind of evening.'

Once again temptation pulled at her but this time she pulled back. 'No, thank you.'

His eyes gleamed with exasperation. 'What happened to the sweet, trusting girl who drank too much champagne and tried to seduce me? She would never have said no to a good night out.'

'She grew up the night you used her to score points over a business rival.' Terrified by her own feelings, she pushed past him but he caught her arm, his fingers holding her still.

'What if my feelings for your father have nothing to do with our conflicting business interests?' He spoke in a tone she'd never heard him use before and it made her pause.

'Of course they do. You're just two alpha males who have to win, and because two people can't both win it's never going to end.'

'Your father ruined my father.' His voice was hoarse and not entirely steady. 'He took everything from him, starting with my mother.'

When Selene simply stared at him, he carried on. 'I was eight years old when Stavros Antaxos landed in his flashy yacht and tempted her away with the promise of a lifestyle beyond her imagination. And just in case she ever changed her mind and considered returning to her husband and son he made sure there was nothing to return to. He destroyed my father's fledgling business, his self-respect and his dignity, and the irony was he didn't need to. The day my mother walked out my father lost everything that mattered to him. He loved her so much that his life had no meaning once she'd gone. So before you judge me remember I have more reason than most for knowing just how low your father will stoop.'

Selene was welded to the spot—and not just by the shock of that unexpected revelation and by the pain she saw in his face. It was the first time she'd seen him display any real human emotion. 'I—I didn't know.'

'Well, now you do.' His tone was flat. His expression blank.

'There have always been women, of course. Before his marriage and afterwards.' She said the words to herself as much as him. 'It was one of the things I hated most— that my mother just accepted it as part of her marriage. I wanted her to have more self-respect, but she was dazzled by him to begin with and then ground down by him. He sucked the personality from her.'

'Yes. That's how he operates.'

'It's driven by insecurity.' She saw it clearly now and wondered why she hadn't before. 'He doesn't believe some-one will stay with him if they can leave, so he stops them leaving. He makes them feel weak. As if they can't survive without him.' And suddenly she knew and the realisation made her feel sick. 'There was a woman—a woman who was in love with him years before my mother ever came on the scene—and she drowned on the rocks off Antaxos.'

He released her suddenly. 'We never knew if it was an accident or if she jumped.'

Without waiting for her to respond he strode away from her, leaving Selene staring after him in appalled silence.

*Your father ruined my father.*

The woman who had drowned was his mother.

'Stefan, wait—*Stefan.*' But her voice was lost in the crowd and he was already out of sight, his long, powerful stride eating up the ground as he walked out of her life, leaving her with nothing but the knowledge she'd been terribly, horribly wrong about him.

# CHAPTER NINE

STEFAN sat sprawled in his chair at the head of the table, his features stony as he listened to his executives discussing a business issue that should have interested him but didn't. His mind was preoccupied with memories he himself had unlocked. It was like ripping open an old wound, tearing through healing tissue and exposing raw flesh. It wasn't just pain, it was screaming agony. But worse than that was the thought of Selene struggling on her own, looking over her shoulder all the time, never able to relax and just enjoy her new life.

Despite the efficient air-conditioning, sweat beaded on his brow.

As well as watching Selene they'd been watching Antaxos but her father hadn't shown his face since their encounter on that day.

What the hell had possessed him to get involved with Stavros Antaxos's daughter? It was a decision that had 'trouble' written all over it.

'Stefan—?'

Hearing his name, he glanced up and saw Maria in the doorway.

It was unheard of for her to interrupt him in a meeting and Stefan rose to his feet in a cold panic. He told himself that Takis would not have let anything happen to Selene, but still his limbs shook as he walked to the door.

'What's wrong? Have you heard from her?' His voice trailed off as he saw Selene standing in his office, the sun sending silver lights shimmering through her newly shorn hair. She wore a simple cotton strap top and a pair of shorts that revealed endless length of tanned leg.

Tears streaked her pretty face.

His world tilted. '*Theé mou*, what has happened?' He was across the room in two strides, his hands on her arms. 'Has he found you? If he's threatened you in some way then I'll—'

'He hasn't threatened me. I haven't seen him.' She choked out the words. Sniffed. 'Nothing like that.'

'Then what the hell is wrong? Tell me.'

The quiet click of the door told him that Maria had left the room, which meant that he was alone with someone who repeatedly made him feel as if he were poised on the top of a slippery slope about to plunge to his doom.

'I was so wrong about you and I'm sorry.' Her eyes lifted to his. 'I— This is *all* my fault. After I met you that night and you were so nice to me I built you up in my head as some sort of hero. I thought about you all the time, I dreamed about you, and then I met you and you were this amazing guy—' Her voice cracked. 'And we had that night, and it was fun, and you were so incredibly sexy, and being in your bed was—well, I just—I never thought anything could feel like that—'

'You need to breathe, *koukla mou.*'

'No, I need to tell you this because I feel *horrible* and I'm not going to stop feeling horrible until I've said what I have to say and you have to listen.'

'I'm listening,' Stefan assured her, 'but I need you

to calm down. I thought you only cried when you were happy?'

'Turns out that's another thing I was wrong about. But mostly I was wrong about you. I was so panicked when I saw those photos, and you were so unconcerned about it I assumed you were responsible. I didn't even think about it from your point of view. Of course you didn't know about my father. Why would you? And I was so used to playing my part in this so-called happy family that I didn't even know how to tell someone that it was all fake.'

'None of this matters now. It's fine.'

'No, it isn't fine. Because you came to that island to rescue me and all I did was yell at you, and then I found out you'd got me the job and had people watching me so that I was safe, but did I thank you?' Her voice rose. 'No! I yelled at you again.'

'You wanted to be independent. I understand that.'

'I was embarrassingly unrealistic. I have no experience, no credentials, nothing that would make an employer take me on, and yet I thought I'd be able to just walk into a job and when I did I didn't even question it. If it hadn't been for you I probably would have been sleeping rough—'

'I've done that and I didn't want it for you.' He wiped that image from his mind.

'You've been so kind to me,' she mumbled, 'and I didn't deserve it. I was mean and I'm not a mean person. But I can see it all more clearly now.'

'You have been through more than anyone should have to. Why would you trust me? I was your father's enemy— that's why you came to me in the first place.'

'But I never saw you as that. I knew you weren't. I knew you were good. You *are* good.' She was standing so close to him he could smell the scent of her hair and see the flecks of black in her green eyes.

'*Don't* start that again.'

'I'm not. I know you're not a hero, but you are good. I also understand now that your mother walking off like that when you were so young must have put you off relationships for life.'

'I have had plenty of relationships.'

'I mean real ones, not just sex. You don't let anyone close because of it and that breaks my heart, because you deserve to have a lovely family.'

Stefan felt a flash of panic. 'Believe me that is *not* what I want. You are far more sensitive about this than I am. It was a long time ago and my mother was just another of your father's many conquests. It happened long, long before he met and married your mother.'

'But you're still hurting. Of course you're hurting. You brush it away like dust on your sleeve but we both know you haven't left it behind. You're carrying it with you into everything you do—your business and your relationships. It's the reason you work so hard and it's the reason you don't get involved with women. It's the reason you don't have a family. You're afraid of losing what you love.'

Her insight shocked him. 'I really don't—'

'I was the one who opened the wound. I pushed you and pushed you and suggested it was just because you were fighting over business—as if you could be that superficial.'

Stefan, who had spent his life being exactly that superficial was floored. 'Selene—'

'I'm sorry.' She flung her arms round him and hugged him tightly.

He stood immobile, the feel of her softness against him driving the breath from his body. And there was that smell again. The smell of her soap that always drove him wild. He closed his eyes and clenched his teeth to try and hold back the rush of feeling.

He couldn't remember being hugged by a woman except as part of foreplay. He stood rigid, unsure what to do next. 'I should probably get back to my meeting.'

'Couldn't they have the meeting without you? We could go somewhere private.' Her voice was muffled in his chest. 'We could have fun and do a few more things on my list.' She was still hugging him, her body warm against his, her arms wrapped around him.

'If we're doing things on your list why do we need to be private?'

'Because most of them involved getting naked with you.'

Stefan gave an incredulous laugh. 'You are the most confusing woman I've ever met.'

'I'm the least confusing woman you've ever met. I'm honest about what I want.'

'And what *do* you want?' He forced himself to ask the question even though he wasn't sure he wanted to hear the answer.

'I want quite a lot. First I'd like you to help me with my business.'

'I thought you didn't want my help?'

'It was incredibly stupid and childish of me to say that. Of course I want your help. I'd be mad to turn it down, wouldn't I? You know more about business than anyone and although candles make you wince I know I have a viable business. But I have no idea how to make it reality. If you're still prepared to help me, I'd be grateful.'

Stefan relaxed slightly. Business was the easy part. 'I'll help you.'

'I'm prepared to work as hard as I have to. I'm excited about it.' Her eyes sparkled. 'I've given up the job in the *taverna*—they only took me on because of you so I felt bad taking a job from someone else. I want to concentrate on my business and if you could loan me enough to live on while I get everything off the ground I'd consider myself fortunate. But I will pay you back. It's a loan, not a gift. No more money tied in a thong.'

Stefan lifted his brows. 'That is a creative way of keeping money in one place.'

'With hindsight it wasn't such a clever idea. My father found it.'

The thought horrified him. 'It's a good job you ran from him when you did.'

'It's a good job you turned up when you did. Thank you for that, too. And I was very impressed that you managed to land a boat on that side of the island without sinking it. That will go down in Antaxos legend, I can tell you.'

'I don't understand how you could have lived with that man all your life and escaped unscathed.'

'I'm not unscathed. I dreamed of heroes. It made me unrealistic. I created a mythical person who could defeat my father and leave him grovelling with apology—' She frowned. 'Come to think of it, you did leave him groveling.'

'But there was no apology.'

'That would have been asking for a miracle.' Her hand was resting on his chest. 'Aren't you going to ask me what else I want apart from help with my business?'

'Go on.'

'I want to be with you. I want to go on dates like normal people. I want to have lots of sex.'

Stefan breathed deeply. 'You shouldn't say things like that—'

'I'm just saying it to you. I know I'm asking a lot because you don't normally date women. This is the part where you tell me you'll break my heart, you don't want happy-ever-after and that the longest relationship you've ever had lasted three courses over dinner.' Her arms slid round his neck. 'And this is the part where I tell you I just want to have fun with someone I trust. I want to explore the chemistry with someone I feel safe with. I want to make love with you the way we did that night at the villa and this time I don't want to have to rush off in the morning.'

Heat spread through his body. 'Selene—'

'But if you'd rather go back to your meeting...' Her finger trailed down his neck. 'Or if being hugged is making you uncomfortable and you'd rather go back to living your life in an isolated bubble, that's fine with me. Actually it's not fine with me, and if that's what you decide you'll probably find I'm just as persistent as you are when I want something.'

He caught her hand in his. 'You're driving me crazy.'

'Good. Because I haven't slept since that night at your villa. I've turned into a sex maniac. If you could do something about that, I'd appreciate it.' Her fingers tangled with his. 'Look at it this way—if it doesn't work out you can just dump me and move on. Isn't that what you always do? It's never caused you a problem before. What's different this time?'

His collar was constricting his throat and he extracted himself from her arms, yanked at his tie and flipped open the top button of his shirt. 'Your first instinct was probably the right one. You should stay away from me. I'm not good for you.'

'Maybe you are. And maybe I'm good for you. But if we don't do this we'll never find out.'

'I know that this product is special. It's a luxury. A treat. Something to make a woman feel pampered. If we sell it in supermarkets as an everyday item, it loses its appeal. It's a high-end product. I thought maybe if we made it exclusive to your spa hotels to begin with it might add to the feel that this is a superior product.'

Selene stopped talking, aware of the twelve people in the room all watching her. It should have felt daunting, but only one person interested her and that was the man who lounged at the head of the table. Stefan hadn't spoken a word since the meeting began and yet it was obvious from the body language of everyone in the room that his opinion was the one that mattered.

He'd removed his jacket. On the surface he was no different from anyone else, and yet he throbbed with authority and power. Even without speaking he commanded the room and Selene felt something stir inside her.

He was shockingly handsome, those dark lashes framing eyes that looked at her with raw sexual promise.

Imagining that mouth on hers, she lost the thread of her speech.

He smiled, and the fact that he so clearly knew what she was thinking infuriated her and at the same time made her insides turn to jelly.

She didn't want to be that predictable, but she loved the fact he could read her. She didn't want him to be so sure of her, but she wanted him to know her. She wanted that intimacy.

'Exclusive,' she said firmly. 'That's the approach I think we should take. By making it hard to get, people might want it more.'

His eyes held hers. Amusement danced there, along with something infinitely darker and more dangerous.

There was an expectant silence. Heads turned to Stefan and finally he stirred.

'It's a high-risk strategy but I like it. Put it into five of our hotels to test it and if it's successful we'll roll it out across the whole group.'

Selene felt the tension ooze out of her. She'd presented her ideas to a commercial task force put together by Stefan and they'd discussed everything from packaging options and advertising to demographics and market forces until her brain was a blur.

'Start exclusive.' Adam, head of Ziakas Business Development, picked up one of the candles and nodded. 'I can work with that. Jenny?'

Jenny was head of public relations for the Ziakas Corporation. 'Yes, our campaign should focus on the luxury element. We'll invite a few journalists for pamper days—they can share their experiences. Spread the word. Create demand. I'll have some companies pitch ideas.'

By the time the meeting eventually finished Selene had been on her feet for almost four hours, but she'd learned so much and her head was buzzing.

'We're done here.' Stefan rose to his feet, dismissing everyone, but as Selene closed her laptop—her brand-new laptop—he stopped her. 'Not you.'

Finally the room cleared and it was just the two of them left alone.

'So...' Stefan strolled round the table, his attention focused on her. 'By making it hard to get, people might want more? I can confirm that's the case. Do you have any idea how much control I had to exercise today?'

Shaken by the look in his eyes, she swallowed. 'Did you?'

'Yes. Normally I like to pace during a meeting. Sitting still drives me mad.'

'So why did you?'

'Because you look disturbingly hot in your suit and I've been aroused for the entire meeting. *Not* comfortable.' He slid his hand behind her neck and drew her face to him. 'Are you wearing stockings under that skirt?'

'Maybe. Possibly.' Her heart was pounding. 'So you would have said yes to anything? Does that mean you thought my ideas were rubbish?'

'No. It means I thought your ideas were excellent but you talk too much.' His eyes were on her mouth. 'You had me sold in the first ten minutes. You could have stopped then and I could have taken you to bed and avoided this prolonged torture.'

'I needed to convince the rest of your team.'

'You only needed to convince me. I'm the one who counts. And now I've had enough of talking about candles.' His eyes gleamed. 'I'm all burnt out.'

'Very funny. Are you laughing at me?'

'I never laugh at business. You have a good product. A product you believe in. You should be proud, *koukla mou.*'

'You shouldn't call me that when we're working. I don't want people to think this is favouritism.'

'I don't care what people think, but just for the record I can tell you that everyone who works for me knows I'm incapable of favouritism.' He slid his fingers into her cropped hair. 'I like it like this.'

'So do I. It was a bit of an impulse but now I've got used to it I think it suits the new me.' She was so aware of him, her body stirring at the memories of how it felt to be with him, and her heart went crazy as he curved his hand around her face and kissed her gently.

'Pack up your things. We're leaving on a market research trip.'

'What sort of market research?'

'You want to sell your product in my exclusive hotels. You've never even stayed in one. So we're going to take your Seduction candle to a hotel and see how it performs in a field test.'

She gave a gurgle of laughter. 'Where?'

'Santorini. You once told me you didn't know Greek Islands could be beautiful. I'm going to broaden your education. It's time you experienced sex against a backdrop of dramatic views and spectacular sunsets.'

'What? Right now?'

'Yes, now. We're going to spend time alone together. Just me, you—' he kissed the top of her nose '—and your candle.'

'And my soap. Don't forget the soap. It's a useful addition to the range.'

'How can I forget the soap?' His hands slid into her hair and his mouth hovered close to hers. 'I smell it on you and it drives me crazy because it makes me think of you naked in my shower.'

'You have a focused mind, Mr Ziakas.'

'I do indeed. And right now it's focused on you.'

They flew to Santorini in his private jet and Selene was dazzled by her first views of the stunning volcanic island with its pretty whitewashed houses and blue-domed churches overlooking the sparkling Aegean Sea.

'It's stunning. I didn't even know places like this existed.'

'Did you never travel anywhere with your father?'

'No. He liked to give the impression of being loving and protective, keeping us out of the media glare, but in reality he just didn't want us to cramp his style. I think he probably stayed in places like this all his life, but without us.'

'This' was the Ziakas Hot Spa, an exclusive hotel consisting of individual private suites nestling into the hillside overlooking the Caldera.

'I never imagined anywhere as romantic as this existed,' Selene murmured as she walked onto their private terrace and stared across the sea.

'You surprise me. Your brain appears to have infinite capacity for dreaming.'

'I know. It's what kept me sane. But this...' She sighed happily and picked up a card from the table placed in a strategic position overlooking the sea. 'This place even has...' She read the card and looked at him in astonishment. 'A pillow menu?'

'Duck as the starter, goose as the main, hypo-allergenic for dessert.' Smiling, he stripped off and dived into their private pool, soaking Selene in the process.

She stood there, gasping, showered in droplets. 'Thank you. Now I'm wet.'

'Good. Join me.'

'We're in public.'

'We are not in public. This is their best suite and it isn't overlooked. And I am the boss.' He gave her a slow, wicked smile. 'No one will dare disturb us, and if they do you have a choice of over seven different pillow types with which to assault them. Are you going to join me voluntarily or do I have to fetch you?'

She put down the pillow menu. 'This is my work suit. It's wet.'

'I'll buy you another. You have to the count of three to get naked. One—'

'But—'

'Two—'

Selene toed off her shoes and wriggled out of her skirt and jacket.

Stefan groaned as he saw her stockings. 'You're killing me.'

'Good.' She slid the stockings down her legs slowly, enjoying his reaction. 'By the way, I'm keeping my underwear on.' As she held her breath and jumped in she thought she heard him mutter 'Not for long...' but the cool water closed over her head and felt blissful on her heated skin.

She surfaced to find him right next to her.

His hand was on her hip and then her waist, and a fierce stab of excitement shot through her body and pooled in her pelvis.

*I love you.*

The words flew into her brain but for once she managed to stop her thoughts popping out through her mouth because she knew this one would send him running.

Instead she stayed still and savoured the contrast between the cool of the water and the heat of his mouth.

She was here. She had now.

That was enough.

Behind them, the setting sun was dipping down to the sea, but neither of them noticed the spectacle that drew tourists from all over the world. Their focus was on each other.

Her mouth was as urgent as his, her hands as desperate to touch and explore, and this time it was all the more exciting because she used the knowledge he'd given her. When she ran her tongue along the seam of his sensual mouth he groaned and tried to take possession, but she held back just a little bit, enjoying the feeling of power that came from knowing she was driving him crazy. But holding back only worked as long as he allowed it, and when he clamped his hand on the back of her head and held her for his kiss it was her turn to moan. His kiss was deliberate and unashamedly erotic, each skilled slide of his tongue a tantalising promise of things to come.

When he closed his hands over her bottom and lifted her she instinctively wrapped her legs around him. Her sensitive skin brushed against his solid, muscular thighs and she realised she was naked—that somehow in the heat of that kiss he'd removed the last of her clothing and she hadn't even noticed. But she noticed now, felt the heat of him brush against her, and the contrast drove her crazy. She dug her fingers into his shoulders, felt resistance and hard muscle beneath sleek bronzed skin.

'I want you.' His eyes were so dark they were almost black, his voice a low growl. 'Here. Now.'

Maybe had she been more coherent she would have worried about the danger of being spotted, but she was beyond caring and simply moved her hips against him in a desperate attempt to relieve the ache between her thighs.

When his hand slid between her legs she gasped against his mouth. The gasp turned to a moan as his fingers explored her with all the intimate knowledge that had driven her wild the first time. His breathing was harsh and shallow, tension etched in his features as he turned her mindless.

And then he shifted her slightly and surged into her. He was hot, so hot in contrast to the cool water, and it felt so impossibly good that she sucked in air and stopped breathing.

*'Cristos—'* His voice was hoarse, his mouth warm on her neck as he struggled to breathe, too. 'You feel—'

'Don't stop. Please, Stefan—' The need in her was so primal she could do nothing but move her hips.

With a soft curse his fingers tightened on her, his grip almost painful. 'Just—wait—'

'Can't—' Eyes closed, she arched into him, took him deeper if that were possible, and he groaned and gave in to it.

He felt smooth, hard, powerful, and the excitement spread through her until there wasn't a single part of her body that couldn't feel him. She tried to rock her hips but his hands were clamped on her, holding her, limiting her movements, so that he was the one who controlled the rhythm. He was merciless with each stroke until the orgasm ripped through her and she sucked in gasping breaths, only dimly aware that he was gripped in his own fierce climax. And then his mouth was on hers and he kissed her through the whole wild experience, swallowing her cries, her gasps, words she wanted to speak but couldn't until the whole thing was nothing but a blur of sexual pleasure.

And when it was over, when her body finally stopped shuddering, he cupped her face in his hands, staring down at her with a stunned look in his eyes.

'That was—'

'Incredible,' she muttered and he lowered his head and kissed her. But it was a gentle, lingering kiss designed to soothe not seduce.

'I don't know what you do to me—'

'You were the one doing it to me—you wouldn't let me move.'

'I didn't dare.' He caught her lower lip gently between his teeth, his eyes fixed on hers. 'You are the sexiest woman I've ever met.'

'You better not have lied about the fact we're not overlooked or I just might turn into the most self-conscious woman you've ever met.'

He closed his hands around her waist and lifted her easily onto the side of the pool. 'Let's take a shower. I think it's time to put in an order from the pillow menu.' He vaulted out of the pool after her, water streaming from his bronzed, powerful shoulders.

It was impossible not to stare and of course he caught her staring. *'Don't* do that.' Snatching a towel from the nearest sun lounger, he pulled her to her feet and wrapped it around her. 'I have to— I can't think when you're naked—'

She was about to ask why he wanted or needed to think but his hand was in his hair and he was clearly striving for some semblance of control.

'You're incredible.' She could say that, surely, without freaking him out? It wasn't what was in her heart but it was all she dared say at this stage. Apparently it was the right thing because he scooped her off her feet and carried her through to the bedroom.

'I'll demonstrate just how incredible—'

She giggled and tightened her grip on him. 'You're going to do your back in.'

'It's not my back I'm worried about. It's other parts of me.'

'Really? Because I might be able to help you with that.' She slid her arms round his neck and pressed her lips to the damp skin of his throat. Then she lifted her head and looked around the bedroom, with its glorious views over the sea. 'I love it here. I could stay forever.'

She felt the change in him. Felt it ripple through him as he lowered her to the ground.

'Why don't you take the first shower? While you're doing that I'll check my e-mails.'

His tone was a shade cooler. Another person probably wouldn't have noticed but she was so tuned in to every subtle shift in her father's moods that she sensed the change instantly.

Confused, she stood for a moment clutching the towel, watching as he strolled to the bed and pulled his phone out of his abandoned trousers.

A moment ago he'd been focused on her and now his focus was on his phone. His business. His world. He'd shut her out as clearly as if he'd closed a door between them.

And she didn't understand it.

Selene cast her mind back to try and work out what

she'd said. 'I love you' had stayed firmly in her head, so it definitely hadn't been that.

All she'd said was that she loved it here so much she could stay forever. And that couldn't possibly—

*Forever.*

Her head snapped up and she stared at the ceiling, wondering how she could have been so stupid. She'd used the word 'forever' and it had to be his least favourite word in the English language.

The fact that it had been a throwaway comment didn't make a difference. It had triggered alarm bells and he'd backed off—withdrawn as quickly as if she'd booked the church. And now his attention was focused on his e-mails as if their steamy, erotic encounter in the pool had never happened.

Selene took a step towards him, then changed her mind and instead walked quietly into the shower and closed the door.

If she brought it up, tried to talk about it, she would just make it worse.

She understood that he was running from attachment. She understood that he kept his relationships short and superficial. She knew all that so it wasn't fair of her to feel this sick disappointment, was it? She knew *him.*

Reminding herself of that, she hit the buttons on the shower. There was an assortment of expensive, exclusive bath products but she ignored them and reached for a bar of her own soap from the bag she'd packed. *Relax,* she thought numbly, letting the scent of it flow over her and into her. It was what she needed.

And tomorrow she'd give him some space.

Show him she wasn't going to crowd him.

# CHAPTER TEN

STEFAN lay in the dark, wide awake as she slept. She'd fallen asleep snuggled next to him and now one slender arm was wrapped around his waist and her head was buried in his shoulder as she breathed softly.

The scent of her soap—*that smell that he associated only with her*—slid into his brain and blurred his thinking.

He wanted to extract himself from her grip but he didn't want to risk waking her.

The night was warm but he was cold with panic.

He shouldn't have brought her here. He'd sent out all the wrong messages and then compounded it by not even waiting for her to undress before having sex with her in the pool.

The intensity of it made him uncomfortable. He was used to being in control, not losing control. He was used to walking away. Used to keeping himself separate. And yet here he was, his limbs tangled with hers, anything but separate.

Tomorrow, he promised himself as he stared into the darkness, when she woke he'd make some excuse. Take her back to Athens and explain he couldn't mix business with pleasure.

Having decided on that approach, he fell asleep—and

woke hours later to find the sun blazing into the room and the bed empty.

'Selene?' Assuming she was in the bathroom, he called her name, but there was no response. He sprang from the bed, prowled out to the terrace area and found no sign of her.

Alarm flashed through him and he reached for his phone and called hotel security, who told him that Selene had been in the hotel spa since it had opened.

Slightly unsettled by just how relieved he felt hearing that, Stefan relaxed and decided to take the opportunity to work. No doubt she was enjoying a massage or something similar and would be back shortly. Then they'd have the conversation he'd been planning. He'd emphasise that this was just fun, not anything serious, and they'd go from there.

Hours later he started to worry that she still hadn't returned.

He was about to call the spa when the door opened and Selene walked back into the suite, wearing a pristine white uniform presumably supplied by the staff of the spa.

His eyes slid to her wonderful curves. 'Where have you been? You've been gone all day.'

'I've been working. Wasn't that why we came here? Market research?' She put her bag down on the sun lounger and slid off her shoes—white pumps that had obviously been provided along with the uniform. 'I've spent the day in the spa, talking to the staff and the customers. It's been so useful. They loved the candles, by the way, and the whole approach of exclusive seems to work for them.' She ran her hands through her hair. 'It's so hot. I'm going to change out of my uniform and then take a dip in the pool.'

'Selene—'

'And I wanted to talk to you.' Her hands were on the buttons of her dress and he felt heat whoosh through him.

This was it.

This was the moment when she talked about the future. Where she tried to turn today into tomorrow and the day after.

'Selene—'

'I felt really strange talking to them about business when they know I'm sharing your suite. It doesn't feel professional. So I propose we end the personal side of our relationship right now. It's been fun, but we don't want to ruin everything.' She poured herself a glass of iced water from the jug on the table. 'Do you want water? I'll pour you some. It's important to drink in this heat and, knowing you, you've been working so hard you've forgotten to drink.'

'End our relationship?' Having planned to suggest exactly the same thing, Stefan was thrown by how badly he didn't want to do that. 'Why would you want to end our relationship?'

'Because I want to be taken seriously in business and that isn't going to happen if I'm having sex with the boss.'

'I don't like hearing you describe it in those terms.'

'Why not? I'm just describing exactly the way it is.'

She drained her glass and he found himself staring at her throat. And lower.

'It isn't awkward and I'm not your boss. You don't work for me. I'm simply investing in your business. It's different.' He wondered why he wasn't just jumping through the escape hatch she'd opened and perhaps she did, too, because she looked surprised.

'It's not that different. I just don't want things to be awkward.'

'I don't have that word in my vocabulary. I do what

suits me and if people don't like it that's their choice.' He watched as she lowered the glass.

'I wasn't talking about things being awkward with other people. I was talking about being awkward between us.' She put the empty glass down on the table. 'It was fun, but I think we should call it a day. Move on.'

'Well, I don't.' Furious, almost depositing his laptop on the terrace, Stefan rose to his feet, dragged her into his arms and kissed her. Her mouth was soft and sweet and the more he tasted, the more he wanted. Desire clawed at him, brutal and intense, driving out every thought he'd had about cutting the threads of this relationship. Usually he was wary of anything that threatened his sense of purpose, but in this case she'd *become* his purpose. He lifted his head. 'You're not moving on. *We're* not moving on.'

She looked dazed. Dizzy. 'I—I assumed that was what you wanted.'

*So had he.* 'Well, it isn't.'

He wondered if 'moving on' meant seeing other men. The thought had him scooping her up and taking her back to bed.


He was a mass of contradictions, she thought days later as she sat across from him in the pretty restaurant that overlooked the bay and the sunset. She'd been so sure that he'd been freaked out when she'd said the word 'forever' and she'd intentionally stayed out of his way, giving him space, only to return and have him behave as possessively as if their relationship were serious.

She wondered if she'd overreacted. If she'd imagined it.

Candles flickered in the faint breeze and sounds of Greek music played in the background.

It felt so far from her old life. 'Has anyone heard anything of my father?'

Stefan frowned. 'You don't need to be worried about your father.'

'I just wondered. I know you're in constant touch with Takis.'

'Of course. He's my head of security.'

'And you briefed him to tell you where my father is at all times.'

'He told you that?'

'He didn't want me to keep looking over my shoulder and worrying.'

Stefan hesitated and then reached for his wine. 'Your father hasn't left Antaxos since that night, although he did have a visit from the police.'

'He will have seen more photographs of us together.'

'But he hasn't acted. He knows he can't touch you. I won't let him touch you.'

The savage edge to his tone shocked her. 'You're so angry with him. Is it because of your mother?'

'No. My mother was an adult. She made a choice and left of her own free will.' He frowned into his glass. 'It took me years to see that.'

'That must have been painful.'

'Because I had to come to terms with the fact she chose him over my father and me? Yes, it was painful. I'd spent years planning how I could become more powerful so that I could storm the island and free her. It took me too long to realise she wouldn't have wanted to be freed.'

That was what had driven him, she realised. He'd wanted power. He'd wanted to be able to wield whatever power he needed.

'But you're still angry—'

'I'm angry because of the way he treated you.' Slowly, he put the glass down on the table. 'My mother had a choice. You didn't. You were trapped there.'

His words warmed her and confused her.

They suggested he cared and yet she knew he avoided that degree of emotional attachment to anyone. She wondered if he was driven by guilt. If he was still blaming himself for exposing her to danger.

She didn't dare hope it was anything else and she certainly didn't dare ask him.

She was just enjoying the moment, and if a part of her wanted it to be more than a moment—well, she ignored it.

She had now. She had him.

'But you rescued me.' Ignoring the envious glances of the other women in the restaurant, Selene lifted her glass. 'I can't believe you're giving me champagne after last time. You swore you'd never do it again.'

'You can drink it as long as you're with me.' His fingertips slowly caressed her wrist and she felt his touch right through her body.

It terrified her that she felt like this. It made her vulnerable, she realised. For her, this had moved beyond fun. It was the most intense experience of her life and the thought of losing it was terrifying.

'It seems ages ago,' she murmured, 'that night at your villa.'

'A lot has happened since then.' His eyes were on hers and then on her mouth and she knew he wanted exactly what she wanted.

'Stefan—'

'Let's go.' Without releasing her hand, he flung money down on the table and propelled her out of the restaurant, either oblivious or indifferent to the interested looks of the other diners.

He released her hand just long enough to ease his car out of its parking space and then slid his fingers into hers again and pressed her hand to his knee, driving one handed through the narrow streets. She probably should have been worried, but the only thing she could focus on was the hardness of his thigh under her hand and the firm grip of his fingers as they held hers.

Her breathing grew shallow. She tried not to look at him but lost the battle and turned her head briefly at the exact time he turned to look at her. Their eyes clashed. Their gazes burned and he cursed softly and brought the car to a ragged halt outside the hotel.

Throwing the keys to the parking attendant, Stefan strode directly to their suite.

They were barely through the door before his hand came behind her neck and he was kissing her.

Mouths fused, they stumbled back and the door slammed shut.

He braced one hand against the door, his other hand holding her face for his kiss, and she wanted it so badly, was so desperate for his touch, his kiss, his body, that her fingers fumbled on the buttons of his shirt. She tore it, sent buttons flying, slid her hands down hard, male muscle and then dragged her mouth from his and kissed her way down his bronzed chest.

She heard the breath hiss through his teeth as she moved lower. Heard him swear softly as she flipped open the button of his trousers, slid the zip and freed him.

She ran her hands over him, loving his body, savouring each moment as she took him in her mouth, first the tip and then as much of him as she could. He gave a harsh groan, both hands braced against the doorframe, as she explored him with the same intimacy with which he'd explored her.

'Selene—' His voice was ragged, his hands unsteady as he lifted her, kissed her hard and backed her towards the bed.

They fell, rolled, and rolled again until she was straddling him. He slid her skirt up her thighs, his hands urgent, his eyes dark with raw need as he wrenched her panties aside. She lowered herself fractionally, held his gaze as she paused and then took him in, took him deep, felt her body accommodate the silken power of him and saw the effort it took him not to thrust, to stay in control.

His eyes closed. His jaw tensed. His throat was damp with sweat, his struggle visible in every gorgeous angle of his sexy face, but she didn't want him to struggle against it. She wanted him to let go of that control and she wanted to be the one who made him do it.

'Stefan...' She murmured his name, leaned forward and licked at his mouth, her body hot and tight around his until he moaned and caught her hips in his hands, trying to slow her down.

She grabbed his hands and pushed them upwards, locking them above his head. He could have stopped her, of course. He was infinitely stronger. But either he was past defending himself or he realised how badly she wanted to take charge because he didn't fight her, just let her hold him there as she slid deeper onto his hard shaft.

'Wait—you have to—'

'Can't wait—' She was past waiting, or slowing down, or stopping or anything else, and so was he. When he thrust hard and deep she felt the power of it right through her body, felt the first fluttering of her own release and then his.

They exploded together, the ripple of her orgasm stroking the length of his hard shaft and taking him with her, on and on, until she collapsed on top of him, spent and stunned.

Weak and disorientated, she tried to roll away from him but he curled his arms around her and pulled the covers over them both.

'Where do you think you're going?'

It was the first time he'd held her like this.

The first time their intimacy had continued after sex.

Drugged with happiness, Selene smiled but didn't say anything. She wondered if he even realised what he'd just done. If not, then she didn't want to risk spoiling it by pointing it out.

He cared for her. She was sure of it.

It was true he hadn't actually said that in as many words, but he'd shown it in a million ways. He'd come after her and rescued her from the island. Then, when she'd escaped from him, he'd made sure she was all right. He'd got her a job and had people watching her so that her father couldn't get to her. And when she'd suggested they end their personal relationship and just focus on the business side of things he'd dismissed the idea instantly.

'I think you might just have killed me,' he murmured, turning his head to look at her.

His eyes were a dark, velvety black and she stared at him and felt something shift inside her.

'I love you.' She said it softly, without thinking, and immediately wanted to snatch the words back because he tensed for a second and then lifted his hand and stroked her hair gently.

'Don't say that.'

'Even if I mean it?'

'You don't mean it. You just feel that way because I'm your first lover. And because you had five years to build me up as a hero in your head.'

'That isn't—' She was going to say that wasn't why she loved him, but she didn't want to risk ruining the moment, so she simply smiled and closed her eyes, keeping her thoughts to herself. 'Let's go to sleep.'

But she was awake long after he was, staring into the

darkness, telling herself that if she kept saying it maybe a time would come when he wanted to hear it. When he might even say it back.

After a blissful week at the spa on Santorini they flew back to Athens and Stefan was sucked back into work, spending long hours in the office and travelling while Selene focused all her attention on the launch of her business.

She missed the intimacy of their suite on Santorini, missed the time when they'd been able to focus only on each other. She wondered if he'd suggest going again, but he was buried under work and the next time she flew to one of his hotels she did it alone.

Of course 'alone' never really was alone, because if he couldn't be with her himself then Stefan made sure Takis was with her. Her protection was something he wouldn't delegate to anyone else and she was touched by the evidence of how much he cared for her. It was there in everything. From the way he held her, confided small details of his life growing up, and from the way he made love to her.

But he never said he loved her and had made it clear he didn't want her to say it either.

Two weeks after they'd arrived back from Santorini they were both due to attend a charity ball and she dressed carefully, excited at the prospect of spending a whole evening with him even if it was in the company of other people.

'I've missed you,' she said cheerfully, taking his arm as they walked to the car.

'I've been hideously busy.'

'I know. I've been worried about you.' She saw him frown briefly as he slid into the car after her.

'Why would you be worried?'

'Because you work too hard,' she said softly. 'Because I care about you.'

'You don't have to worry about me.'

'Why not? Presumably you worry about me or you wouldn't arrange for someone to be with me all the time—and not just someone: Takis. It's all part of caring.'

His eyes were fixed straight ahead, his profile rigid and inflexible. 'I put you in danger. It's up to me to make sure you don't suffer for that.'

'That's all it is? Guilt?' Suddenly it upset her that he couldn't at least admit to caring just a little bit. 'You care about me, Stefan, I know you do.'

'We've arrived.' His tone cool, he unsnapped his seat belt and opened the door even though the car had barely come to a halt.

Exasperated, Selene started to speak, but he was already out of the car and standing on the red carpet waiting for her while the paparazzi crowded together to take photographs.

More photographs, she thought dully. More photographs of another fake life. Another evening where she had to pretend that what was on the surface reflected reality. Another evening of lies and never saying what she really felt. Fortunately this was her particular area of expertise, so she smiled dutifully, held his hand, posed for photographers, ate a reasonable quantity of her meal, listened attentively to speeches and did everything she was expected to do—just as she had for her father.

And all the time she felt numb inside.

'Do you want to dance?' Stefan rose to his feet and frowned when she didn't respond. 'Selene?'

She rose automatically. 'Yes, of course.'

His eyes narrowed on her face but she ignored him and walked onto the dance floor, then stopped dead. 'Actually, no.'

'No?' He drew her into his arms but she stayed rigid.

'I can't do this.'

'I thought you'd enjoy it, but if you don't want to dance you just have to say so.'

'Not the dancing. All of it.' She lifted her eyes to his. 'I can't be fake any more. I won't live a false life. I've done it for as long as I can remember and it stops now. This is who I am. This is what I feel. I'm not going to hide any more.'

His expression was guarded. 'Hide what?'

'The way I feel about you.' The look in his eyes should have silenced her instantly but she was beyond being silenced. 'I tiptoed round a man for twenty-two years of my life, Stefan, watching every word I said, trying not to upset him. I won't live like that again. I want to be able to express how I feel without worrying that I'm upsetting the person I'm with.'

His eyes darkened. 'Are you suggesting I'd hurt you?'

His interpretation shocked her. 'No, of course not. But the fact that you don't want me to tell you how I feel is making me miserable.'

'You're miserable?'

'Yes,' she whispered. 'Yes, I am. Because I love you and you don't want to hear it. I have to bite my tongue and squash everything I'm feeling down inside and I hate that.'

He didn't answer her. Just stared at her in silence while the couples around them moved slowly on the dance floor.

And suddenly she realised she'd done it again. She'd created something in her head out of nothing. When was she going to realise that just because she wanted something to happen it didn't mean she could think it into happening?

She could want him to open up, but that didn't mean he ever would.

And she could live with that or she could make a different choice.

A choice that didn't need her to compromise everything that mattered to her.

Music flowed around her but all she was aware of was him and the huge pain pressing down on her chest. 'I can't do this…' Her words were barely audible but clearly he heard her because his face seemed set in stone. 'I can't be with a man who is afraid to feel. And I can't be with a man who doesn't want to hear how I feel. I thought I could, but I can't. I'm sorry.' Mumbling the words, she pulled away from him. 'I hope you find someone. I really do. I want that for you.'

Heart breaking, knowing she had to get away before she made a terrible fool of herself, she forged her way through the crowded dance floor, slipped through a side door into a carpeted corridor and walked slap into her father.

'Hello, Selene.'

Her legs turned to water. Seeing him here was the last thing she'd expected. Since she'd been with Stefan she'd stopped looking over her shoulder. Behind her she could hear music from the dance floor, but this part of the corridor was empty and he was between her and the only exit. 'I didn't know you were here.'

'So you're still trying to make a fool of me?'

'I'm not trying to make a fool of you. I'm just living my life.'

'You came here in public with that man. He is setting you up in business. How do you think that looks to people? My biggest competitor sponsoring my daughter in her pathetic business venture.'

It was always about him, she thought dully. Always about his public image. Never about anyone else.

'It has nothing to do with you and the only reason I had to ask him is because you wouldn't help me. This is my business and it isn't pathetic. It's real. That's why he's helping me. He's sees the potential.'

'Potential?'

His laughter made Selene flinch.

This was what had drained her mother's confidence. The consistent drip of derision that eroded like acid.

For the past month she'd lived in a protected bubble. She'd forgotten what it felt like to be put down all the time. She'd forgotten how it felt to watch every word she spoke and feel her way through every conversation. 'He's helping me because I have a really good business idea that is going to make him money.'

'You're still as naïve as ever. His only interest in you is as a weapon to strike me.'

'Why do you always think everything is about you?' The words flew from her mouth and she immediately clamped it shut, cursing herself for not thinking before she spoke. Once it had been second nature to do that but with Stefan she spoke freely about everything. Well, everything except one thing. The most important thing. And she couldn't think about that now.

As always her father pounced on weakness. 'Has he ever said he loves you?'

As always he picked the words designed to do maximum damage. To inflict maximum pain.

His timing was so perfect this time she even wondered if he'd somehow overheard their exchange on the dance floor. No. He couldn't have done. If he'd been anywhere near the dance floor she would have seen him.

Or would she?

She'd been so wrapped up in her own misery she hadn't been paying attention to anyone around her.

'What Stefan says or doesn't say to me is none of your business.'

'In other words he *hasn't* told you he loves you. And now you're fooling yourself that he will say it given time.'

'I won't talk about this with you.'

'He's using you. And when he's got what he wants he'll dump you just as he's dumped every woman before you. Women are a short-term distraction, nothing more.'

She had no intention of telling him she'd just ended it.

'Don't you even care?' Horrified, she heard her voice crack. 'You're supposed to be my father. You're supposed to love me and want me to be happy. Instead you only ever smile when my life is falling apart. It pleases you that I'm unhappy.'

'If you're unhappy then it's your own fault.' There was no sympathy in his face. 'If you'd stayed at home with your family instead of destroying it, your life wouldn't be falling apart.'

'I did *not* destroy our family! You did that.'

'You are a hopeless dreamer. You always have been. You're a sitting duck for the first guy who comes along and shows you some attention.'

'That is enough.' A cold, hard voice came from behind her and Selene turned to see Stefan standing there in all his powerful fury, that angry gaze fixed on her father. 'You don't speak to her again—ever.'

'And why would you care, Ziakas? You used her.'

'No. It was you who used her. You used her to project the image of a happy family but you've never been a father to her. And I care because I love her and I won't let you upset someone I love.'

Selene couldn't breathe.

She'd wanted so badly to hear him say those words. Even though she knew he'd only said it to protect her from her father, she felt something twist inside her.

There was a long silence and then her father laughed. 'You don't believe in love any more than I do.'

'Don't bracket us together.' Stefan's voice was pure ice. 'I am nothing like you.' He took her hand, his touch firm and protective as he drew her against him. 'Let's go. There's nothing for you here.'

Stefan steered her through the crowd and down into the gardens. She was pale and unresponsive, walking where he led her but not paying any attention. Only when he was sure they were in private did he stop walking and that was when he saw the tears.

Her face was streaked with them, her eyes filled with a misery so huge that it hurt him to look at it.

'He's not worth it.' He cupped her face in his hands, desperate to wipe away those tears while everything inside him twisted and ached just to see her so unhappy. 'He isn't worth a single tear. Tell me you know that. *Theé mou*, I wish I'd punched him again just for having the nerve to approach you.'

'He waited until I was alone.'

'Like the coward he is.' Seriously concerned, he gathered her close, hugged her tightly. 'I had no idea he was even here or there is no way I would have let you walk away from me. Takis is here, but because you were with me—'

'I can protect myself. I've done it my whole life.'

'And the thought of you alone with him, growing up with him, horrifies me. I can't bear to think of it.'

'You grew up alone. That's worse.'

'No. It was easier. All I had to do was move forward. You had to escape before you could do that. Every time I think about how I messed that up I go cold.'

'It was my fault for not telling you. Don't let's go over that again.' She eased out of his grasp and brushed the heel of her hand over her cheeks. 'Sorry for the crying. I know you hate it.'

'Yes, I hate it—I hate seeing you unhappy. I never want

to see you unhappy.' He realised that he'd do anything, *anything*, to take those tears away.

'Thank you for what you said in there. For standing up for me when he said all those awful things about you just being with me to get back at him.'

When he thought of the contempt in her father's eyes he felt savage. Shocked by the extreme assault of emotion, he pushed aside his own feelings and concentrated on hers. 'What he said wasn't true. You do know that, don't you? Tell me you're not, even for a moment, thinking to yourself that he might have been right.'

'I'm not thinking that. I know what we had was real.'

The fact that she put it in the past tense sent a flash of panic burning through him. 'It *is* real.'

But she wasn't listening. 'He called my business pathetic.'

'He will eat those words when he sees the success of your business, *koukla mou*. And he *will* see it.'

'Thank you for believing in me. You're the first person to ever do that. Even my mother didn't think I could do it.'

'But you believed in yourself. You came to me with your candles and your soap and the beautiful packaging you'd made yourself. You are *so* talented. Your business idea is clever and you work harder than anyone on my team. If you weren't already making a success of being an entrepreneur, I'd employ you straight away.'

Her hand rested on his chest, as if she couldn't quite bear to let him go. 'But you probably wouldn't have offered to help me if I hadn't been who I was.'

'I probably would.' He gave a half-smile. 'I'm a sucker for a woman dressed in a nun's costume.'

There was no answering smile and he was shaken by how badly he missed that ready smile. He'd taken it for granted. She was always so bouncy and optimistic and yet now she just stood there, shivering like a wounded animal.

'Selene—'

'I should go. Someone might see me and take a photograph.' Finally she smiled, but it was strained. 'See? I'm learning. I don't want my father knowing he made me cry. That's one act I'm prepared to keep up until the day I die.' She rubbed her hand over her face again. 'It was kind of you to come to my defence. Kind of you to tell him our relationship meant something.'

'It wasn't kindness.' He'd realised it the moment she'd walked away from him. 'I do love you.'

'Yes, I know.' There was no pleasure in that statement. Her face didn't light up. She just looked incredibly sad. 'I know you do, Stefan. But you don't want to. It scares you.'

'Yes, it does.' He didn't deny it because he knew only honesty would save him now. 'I didn't want it to happen. I've done my best not to let it happen by picking women I couldn't possibly fall in love with. I controlled that.'

'I know that, too. I know *you*.' She eased out of his arms. 'I really do have to go. I don't want anyone taking a photograph of me like this.'

'I'll take you home. Then we'll fly to my villa.' He saw her hesitate and then shake her head.

'No, not this time. I'll see you in the office on Monday. We have the ad agency pitch.'

'I'm not talking about business. I'm talking about us.' It was a word he'd never used before. 'I've just told you that I love you.'

'But you don't want to. You don't want to feel that way and I can't be with a man who always holds part of himself back. Even though I understand all your reasons and I'm sympathetic, I want more. I know love makes a person vulnerable but I want a man who is prepared to risk everything because the love is more important than protecting himself. And I want him to value my love and allow me to express it.'

'Selene—'

'Please don't follow me. Not this time. I'll see you in the office on Monday.' Mumbling the words, she hurried away from him, walking so fast she almost stumbled.

She applied layers of make-up, added blusher, but still she looked pale when she walked into the Ziakas building.

The glamorous receptionist smiled at her. '*Kalimera.* They're all waiting for you in the conference room.'

But when she walked in the room was empty apart from Stefan, who was pacing from one end of the room to the other.

When he saw her, his face paled. 'I was afraid you wouldn't turn up.'

'Why? Today is important.' Horrified by how hard it was to see him, she glanced around the room. 'Where is everyone?'

'I sent them to get breakfast. They're coming back in an hour. I need to talk to you. I need you to hear what I have to say.'

Her heart clenched at the thought of going over it again. 'There really isn't—'

'You were right—I do love you.' Tension was stamped in every line of his handsome face. 'I think I've loved you from the day you walked into my office dressed as a nun, determined to find a way through my security cordon. Or maybe it was before that—maybe a part of me fell in love with the seventeen-year-old you—I don't know.'

She'd never seen him look like this. Never seen him so unsure of himself. 'Stefan—'

'You were so open about your feelings. I'd never met

anyone like you. It frightened me and it fascinated me at the same time. I liked the fact that you spoke openly without guarding every word. It made me realise the other people in my life were—' he frowned as he searched for the word '—fake.'

'So was I.'

'No. I saw *you* that night. The real you. And when you walked into my office that day and pulled out your candles and asked for a loan I was so cynical, so sure I knew everything there was to know about women and had it all under control. I didn't look deeper. I judged you based on everything that had gone before. But the truth was I knew nothing about you. You shook every preconceived idea I had about women. That night when you had too much champagne—'

'You were so kind to me.'

'You have no idea how much self-control it took to keep my hands off you.' He groaned, dragging his fingers through his hair. 'You were sweet and sexy rolled into one and so unbelievably curious—'

'Why was it unbelievable? You're the most gorgeous man I'm ever going to meet. I wanted to make the most of it.'

'When I worked out your reasons for wanting to leave the island I couldn't believe I'd been so blind. I couldn't believe I hadn't worked it out.'

'Why would you? My father can be very persuasive.'

'And I have more reason to know that than most.'

'None of this matters now.'

'No, it doesn't, because you're mine now and I'm never letting you go.' His voice hoarse, he crossed the room in three strides and took her face in his hands. 'Until I met you all I knew about love was how much damage it could do. I didn't want that. I spent my life avoiding that.

I couldn't understand why anyone would take that risk and I certainly didn't want to, so I kept my relationships short and superficial—and then I met you and suddenly I didn't want to do either of those things. For the first time ever I cared whether I saw a woman again. I wanted to see you again.'

'And you were scared.'

'Yes, and you knew that. You knew I was scared. You knew I loved you.'

'I thought you did. I hoped you did. But I never thought you'd admit it. Or want it.'

'I do want it. I want you.'

He kissed her gently, his mouth lingering on hers, and her head reeled and her thoughts tumbled as she tried to unravel the one situation she hadn't prepared for.

'I— It's too complicated. You hate my father.'

'It's not complicated. I'm not marrying your father and I'm hoping you won't want to invite him to our wedding.'

Her heart thudded and skipped. 'Is that a proposal?'

'No. I haven't reached that part yet but I'm getting there. I have something for you.'

He reached for a box on the table and her brows rose because she recognised the packaging.

'That's one of my candles.'

'Close. It's one I had developed just for you. You already have Relax, Energise and Seduction. This one is called Love.'

Love?

He wanted to marry her?

Hands shaking, Selene opened the box and saw a diamond ring nestling in a glass candle-holder. 'I don't know what I'm more shocked about—the fact that you're asking me to marry you or the fact that you've actually given me a candle. Does this mean I'm actually allowed to light it in the bedroom?'

'You can do anything you want with me in the bedroom,' he said huskily, sliding the ring onto her finger and then kissing her again. 'Just don't tell me it's too late. Don't tell me you've given up on me for taking so long to discover what you knew all along.'

'I'm not telling you that. It's not too late. It's never too late.' She stared down at the ring on her finger, hypnotised not just by the diamond but by what it symbolised.

'How did you end up such an optimist with a father like yours?'

'I refused to believe that all men were like my father. I knew they couldn't be—especially after I met you. I believed in something better and I wanted that. Why would someone want to repeat the past when the future can be so much better?'

His lips were on hers. 'You are an inspiration, *koukla mou*.'

'Not really.' She melted under his touch. 'I'm just trying to have the life I want. Which probably makes me horribly selfish.'

'Then we're a perfect match, because you know I don't think of anyone but myself.'

But he was smiling as he said the words and so was she, because the happiness was too big to keep inside.

'You kept shutting me out.'

'You were so affectionate. So open. I kept shutting you out and when you said those words I panicked.'

'I know.'

'I'm not panicking now.' He trailed his fingers down her cheek. 'So any time you want to say them again, that would be good.'

She smiled again. 'What words?'

'Now you're torturing me, but I suppose I deserve it.'

'I'm not torturing you—' she wrapped her arms round his neck '—I just don't know which words you mean.'

'You're a wicked tease.' His mouth was hot on hers and she gasped as he lifted her onto the table.

'Any moment now thirty people are going to walk into this room.'

'Then you'd better say those words fast—unless you want to say them in front of an audience.'

'Which words?'

He cupped her face. 'The ones where you tell me how you feel about me.'

'Oh, *those* words.' She loved teasing him. 'I've forgotten how to say them because you didn't want to hear them. They've vanished from my brain.'

'Selene—'

'I love you.' For the first time she said it freely, and she smiled as she did so because it felt so good to be truly honest about her feelings. No more hiding. No more pretending. 'I really love you and I'll always love you.'

They kissed, lost in each other, until they heard applause and both turned to see a crowd in the doorway led by Maria, who was smiling. Behind her stood Takis, Kostas and all the other members of Stefan's senior team.

Blushing, Selene slid off the table and Stefan muttered under his breath.

'What does a guy have to do to ensure privacy round here?'

'We came to congratulate you.' Maria produced two bottles of champagne which she put on the table and then turned to hug Selene. 'I'm so delighted. I know it's a little early in the day, but we thought it was appropriate to celebrate the occasion with champagne.'

Stefan eyed the bottles with incredulity. 'You shouldn't

even have been aware of the occasion. Were you listening at the door?'

'Yes.' Maria was unapologetic.

Takis eyed his boss cautiously and then slid into the room, put a tray of glasses on the table and hugged Selene, too.

Choked, Selene hugged them both back. 'Thank you for watching over me and being so kind.'

'If everyone could stop hugging my future wife,' Stefan drawled, 'I'd quite like to hug her myself. But it appears I no longer have any influence in my own office.'

'This is a special occasion, boss,' Takis muttered, releasing Selene. 'Some of us had given up on ever seeing this day.'

Unbelievably touched, Selene slid her hand into Stefan's as his executive team piled into the room. 'This is so great! Can we open the champagne? I always wanted to live a champagne lifestyle—although preferably without the headache.'

Takis reached for the nearest bottle. 'Champagne in a breakfast meeting. A typical working day in the Ziakas Corporation.'

Stefan rolled his eyes. 'Clearly you've never seen what happens to Selene when she drinks champagne.'

'I'm lovely when I drink champagne—and anyway I have Takis to extract me from danger.'

'That's *my* job now. I'm signing on full-time.' Stefan pulled her back into his arms and kissed her, ignoring their audience. 'Which is just as well if you intend to go through life with a glass of champagne in your hand.'

She smiled up at him. 'Good things happen when I drink champagne. You know that.'

'Yes.' His eyes glittered into hers. 'I do.'

There was a thud as the champagne cork hit the ceiling,

and Selene beamed as Takis handed her a glass of champagne. 'We have four advertising agencies sitting in the lobby, waiting to pitch to us. They're going to think we're very unprofessional.'

'They can think what they like.' Stefan tapped his glass against hers and bent his head to gently kiss her mouth. 'Just this once I'm mixing business with pleasure.'

* * * * *

# ROMANCE

# MEDICAL

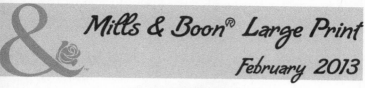

# Mills & Boon® Large Print
## February 2013

# ROMANCE

| | |
|---|---|
| **Banished to the Harem** | Carol Marinelli |
| **Not Just the Greek's Wife** | Lucy Monroe |
| **A Delicious Deception** | Elizabeth Power |
| **Painted the Other Woman** | Julia James |
| **Taming the Brooding Cattleman** | Marion Lennox |
| **The Rancher's Unexpected Family** | Myrna Mackenzie |
| **Nanny for the Millionaire's Twins** | Susan Meier |
| **Truth-Or-Date.com** | Nina Harrington |
| **A Game of Vows** | Maisey Yates |
| **A Devil in Disguise** | Caitlin Crews |
| **Revelations of the Night Before** | Lynn Raye Harris |

# HISTORICAL

| | |
|---|---|
| **Two Wrongs Make a Marriage** | Christine Merrill |
| **How to Ruin a Reputation** | Bronwyn Scott |
| **When Marrying a Duke...** | Helen Dickson |
| **No Occupation for a Lady** | Gail Whitiker |
| **Tarnished Rose of the Court** | Amanda McCabe |

# MEDICAL

| | |
|---|---|
| **Sydney Harbour Hospital: Ava's Re-Awakening** | Carol Marinelli |
| **How To Mend A Broken Heart** | Amy Andrews |
| **Falling for Dr Fearless** | Lucy Clark |
| **The Nurse He Shouldn't Notice** | Susan Carlisle |
| **Every Boy's Dream Dad** | Sue MacKay |
| **Return of the Rebel Surgeon** | Connie Cox |

# Mills & Boon® Hardback

## March 2013

## ROMANCE

| | |
|---|---|
| Playing the Dutiful Wife | Carol Marinelli |
| The Fallen Greek Bride | Jane Porter |
| A Scandal, a Secret, a Baby | Sharon Kendrick |
| The Notorious Gabriel Diaz | Cathy Williams |
| A Reputation For Revenge | Jennie Lucas |
| Captive in the Spotlight | Annie West |
| Taming the Last Acosta | Susan Stephens |
| Island of Secrets | Robyn Donald |
| The Taming of a Wild Child | Kimberly Lang |
| First Time For Everything | Aimee Carson |
| Guardian to the Heiress | Margaret Way |
| Little Cowgirl on His Doorstep | Donna Alward |
| Mission: Soldier to Daddy | Soraya Lane |
| Winning Back His Wife | Melissa McClone |
| The Guy To Be Seen With | Fiona Harper |
| Why Resist a Rebel? | Leah Ashton |
| Sydney Harbour Hospital: Evie's Bombshell | Amy Andrews |
| The Prince Who Charmed Her | Fiona McArthur |

## MEDICAL

| | |
|---|---|
| NYC Angels: Redeeming The Playboy | Carol Marinelli |
| NYC Angels: Heiress's Baby Scandal | Janice Lynn |
| St Piran's: The Wedding! | Alison Roberts |
| His Hidden American Beauty | Connie Cox |

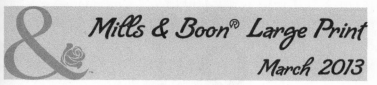

*Mills & Boon® Large Print*

*March 2013*

# ROMANCE